Cora's Kitchen

Cora's Kitchen

To Laura & Ashley
thanks so much for
coming. It was a pleasure
to meet you.
Enjoy,
Kimberly Garrett Brown
'22

KIMBERLY GARRETT BROWN

INANNA poetry
& fiction

Toronto, Ontario, Canada
www.inanna.ca

**Canada Council
for the Arts** **Conseil des Arts
du Canada**

We gratefully acknowledge the support of the Canada Council for the Arts and
the Ontario Arts Council for our publishing program. We also acknowledge the
financial support of the Government of Canada.

Cover design: Val Fullard
Cover art: Janet McClean

Cora's Kitchen is a work of fiction. All names, characters, businesses, places,
events and incidents in this book are either the product of the author's imagination or used in a fictitious manner.

All trademarks and copyrights mentioned within the work are included for
literary effect only and are the property of their respective owners.

Library and Archives Canada Cataloguing in Publication

Title: Cora's kitchen / Kimberly Garrett Brown.
Names: Garrett Brown, Kimberly, author.
Series: Inanna poetry & fiction series.
Description: Series statement: Inanna poetry & fiction
Identifiers: Canadiana (print) 20220274592 | Canadiana (ebook) 20220274606
| ISBN 9781771338516 (softcover) | ISBN 9781771338523 (HTML) | ISBN
9781771339056 (PDF)
Subjects: LCGFT: Novels.
Classification: LCC PS3607.A775 C67 2022 | DDC 813/.6—dc23

Printed and bound in Canada

Inanna Publications and Education Inc.
210 Founders College, York University
4700 Keele Street, Toronto, Ontario, Canada M3J 1P3
Telephone: (416) 736-5356 Fax: (416) 736-5765
Email: inanna.publications@inanna.ca Website: www.inanna.ca

She stands
In the quiet darkness,
This troubled woman
Bowed by
Weariness and pain
Like an
Autumn flower
In the frozen rain,
Like a
Wind-blown autumn flower
That never lifts its head
Again.

— Langston Hughes, "Troubled Woman"
From *The Weary Blues* (1926)

March 29, 1928

The last thing I wanted to do after working all day was traipse around Harlem looking for that boy, but Mr. Peterson called the house again this evening. Junior didn't show up for work for the second time this week. I contemplated waking Earl to go look for him, but he's ornery if he doesn't get a nap before he goes to the club.

I checked the park between our house and the school, but Junior wasn't there. A couple of girls who looked his age told me they talked to him right after school, although they didn't remember which way he went. I searched alleys, basement apartment stairwells and every other hidden corner I could think of until I wound up at Shorty's bar. Young boys like to hang out there because they can drink and gamble. I have told Junior if I ever caught him there, I'd wear his hide out. But he thinks at 13 he's grown.

The place was practically empty, still reeking of musty cigar smoke and alcohol. Three men sitting at a table just inside the door stopped talking when I came in. The floor was so sticky I feared my shoes would get stuck. I walked over to the bar and asked the bartender if he had seen Junior. He hadn't. I turned to leave but noticed the men at the table watching me. One of them, wearing a gray pinstriped suit, nodded as he swirled his glass. I stopped at the table to ask if they had seen Junior even though I knew they wouldn't tell the truth if they had. Of course they said they had not.

On my way out, I recognized a boy from our building. He ducked his head when he saw me. Young folks today don't respect their elders as they did when I was coming up. If someone's mother from the neighborhood was looking for them, I would have spoken up — mostly out of fear that she would tell my mother I hadn't helped. Nowadays, there's no telling how the parents might react if you tell them about their children. It's best to mind your own business unless you know the parents well.

I walked up and down a few more blocks and then to Peterson's Market to see if Junior had shown up. Lo and behold, there he was sweeping the floor behind the counter.

"What you doing down here, Mama?" he asked as if he had been there all along.

I had half a mind to take off my shoe and beat the living daylights out of Junior, but Mr. Peterson was standing next to him.

"Mrs. James, what brings you down here?" he asked.

"I need some collards for dinner," I said.

I bought three bundles of collards so I didn't look like a fool. But I tossed them in the first rubbish bin I passed on my way home because they smelled sour. A quarter wasted. Mr. Peterson ought to be ashamed of himself, selling near-rotten fruits and vegetables for twice as much as you can get at the markets uptown, but he knows no one is going to complain. He's the only market for almost a mile. Most people don't have money or time to search for a better deal. I suppose I shouldn't complain, though. At least Junior has a job.

When I got home, Earl was getting dressed for work. He fussed all through dinner after I told him what happened. Junior was lucky his father left for the club before he got home from work. Hopefully, Earl will have calmed down by the time he sees Junior in the morning.

The whole incident reminded me of the Langston Hughes poem I came across shelving books this afternoon called "Troubled Woman." I cried as I read it. It felt as if Langston was standing in my kitchen watching me hunched over the sink, washing dishes. I'd never thought of myself as a troubled woman before, but I am. My days are becoming more and more wearisome. Sometimes I wonder how I'm going to make it. I copied the poem onto a piece of paper to study when I got home. It makes me want to write, but I don't know where or how to start. It's too bad I can't write like Langston. I sure would have a lot of stories to tell about being a troubled woman.

I wonder how he came up with that idea anyway. If he wasn't away at college, I'd ask him. I miss seeing him at the library forums and the Booklover's Club.

New York, New York
April 2, 1928

Dear Langston,

I read one of your poems a few days ago and thought I would write you a letter. I hope you don't mind.

The library has not been the same since you went away to school. There are still spirited discussions about race issues at the forums and new authors reading at the Booklover's Club meeting, but no one talks about poetry, books or writing the way you and I did over the last year.

I know it sounds odd to say no one talks about books at the library. People have conversations all the time, but they are mostly superficial discussions. Someone will say I loved this or that about a book but then will not be able to describe why. It's like there is no appreciation for the words. No one takes the time to savor the story. A patron came in to return a copy of Walt Whitman's Leaves of Grass. *I asked him what he thought of "Song of Myself," particularly 21, and he responded:* It was nice.

I stood there, astonished. How can you come away from Whitman with "it was nice?" The opening of stanza 21 takes my breath away:

> *"I am the poet of the Body and I am the poet of the Soul,*
> *The pleasures of heaven are with me and the pains of hell*
>   *are with me,*
> *The first I graft and increase upon myself, the latter I*
>   *translate into a new tongue."*

One stanza conveys the urging of the body and the longing of the soul. I feel the complexity of heaven and hell within my own life.

It's a blessing to work at the library surrounded by books and words and ideas. I have a friend who studied to be a teacher, but no school would hire her because she's colored. She works for a white family as a maid. She helps the children with their lessons from time to time, but she will always be more mammy than tutor. So, while there are times I feel more like a clerk

5

than a librarian, I know working here is better than cooking or cleaning for a white woman.

And yet, I don't feel any closer to accomplishing my dreams than my friend is to teaching school. It's as if I'm trapped in purgatory, knowing I want more from life, but unable to do anything about it. Then I feel guilty for not being satisfied. I have a good job, a roof over my head, and a family who loves me. But like Whitman says, "the pains of hell are with me."

When I met my husband, he explained his life would be worthless if he had to give up music. Part of the pain of hell for me is I don't think I'm being who I need to be. If I were, my writing wouldn't be limited to my journal.

All of this comes to the surface when I read those words in Whitman's poetry. It can't be whittled down to simply saying, "It's nice."

Don't feel obligated to write back. Knowing you're reading my letters is enough.

Sincerely yours,

Cora James

April 5, 1928

I can't stop thinking about that poem. The words "quiet darkness" and "troubled woman" keep rumbling through my mind. It's been a few days, and I still haven't heard from Langston. I wonder if he got my letter. What if he's angry and wrote to Mrs. Rose to complain? She will most certainly chastise me for taking such liberties.

I probably would have worked myself into a real lather if Dorothy's huffing and puffing hadn't started to get on my nerves. She has taken to pouting whenever I make her help me in the kitchen.

"You've got a lot of years of cooking ahead of you," I said.

"I'll be too busy taking care of patients," she said.

Her expression reminded me of Mama. They have the same features: almond-shaped eyes, short, flat nose, plump cheeks. The only things missing are the deep lines that were carved into Mama's face and the sadness in her eyes. Time and disappointment do that to you, I guess. Seems like every time I look in the mirror, there are deeper lines in my face.

Truth is, when I was 11 years old, I hated being stuck in the house cooking, too. It didn't seem fair. My brothers got to do whatever they wanted. Of course, I never dared let Mama see me sulking. Laziness was always met with a stern warning from scripture: "By much slothfulness the building decayeth; and through idleness of the hands the house droppeth through."

The only good thing about being in the kitchen with Mama was she loved to tell stories, especially about the beaus who courted her before she married my father. She'd go over every detail, as if she were savoring a piece of rock candy. I once suggested we write down her stories and send them to the *Ladies' Home Journal*.

Ain't nobody interested in stories about a colored woman. Don't let all that reading go to your head, she said, not even bothering to look up from what she was doing.

"You look like my mother," I said as I stood up from the kitchen table.

"I thought you said she looked like Aunt Lucy," Dorothy said, turning up her nose.

"She did, but prettier," I said with a wink.

The redness in Mama's brown skin and her high cheek bones made her look Indian, though she never wanted any part of that side of her family. She used to say she didn't believe in them. I think what she meant was that she didn't believe in their traditions. But she was just like them. Looking to the moon for signs. Blending plants and herbs to cure ailments. Watching animals for predictions.

It's too bad she never got to see any of her grandchildren.

April 6, 1928

I can't sleep. Something has been bothering me since Earl left for work tonight.

I was washing the dishes after dinner. My hair stood straight up on my head like Medusa, droplets of sweat trailing down the side of my face. I looked up and Earl was in the doorway watching me. Tuxedo freshly ironed. The crisp, white collar of his shirt resting against his smooth chestnut neck. Eyes dancing. He came over and pressed his lips into the crook of my neck. His warm breath thawed the tension in my shoulders. But then I thought: *Why is he so happy?*

It made me think of my mother sitting in that rocking chair by the window at night, with her Bible on her lap, waiting for my father to come home from the store. Every now and then I'd catch her glancing at the clock on the wall. The corners of her mouth would turn down as she slowly shook her head. *Lord, have mercy*, she'd say with a loud sigh. I promised myself I would never be sitting up at night waiting for a man, but here I am.

I'm not worried about who he's with or what he's doing. There will always be some temptation for him at the nightclub, but I'd run myself crazy if I didn't trust him. So, I don't think too much about that. What bothers me though is the ease of his life. He goes to work, plays the music he loves, and comes home. The rest is left to me.

What would life be like if I were a writer? Maybe I'd be like Zora Neale Hurston. She strides into the library with such fanfare and confidence. She's not running around Harlem after a hard-headed 13-year-old. What made me think Langston would be interested in my dream of becoming a writer?

Lincoln University
Pennsylvania
April 5, 1928

Dear Cora,

What a wonderful surprise to hear from you. I've been awfully busy here working on a survey for a sociology assignment. The whole thing is causing quite a stir. But I found it so refreshing to hear from you in the midst of it all. So, by all means, please write.

I'm glad you enjoyed reading Whitman. His eye for observation helps me look deeper into my own world. I have used many of his themes as inspiration for my own poems. Of course, if you're interested more in prose than poetry, you may want to look at his collection of notes and essays in *Specimen Days*. Following his example may help you to move beyond journaling. Imagine the observations you could make about people in the library. It is surely a magical place with fascinating people and interesting conversations.

Though a husband and family may make it more difficult to find time to write, you must write if by not writing "the pains of hell are with [you]." If you are looking for motivation, *Opportunity* is sponsoring a short story contest. The deadline is not until the end of August. That gives you a little over four months to write something. The details are on the last page of this month's issue. If you decide to enter one of your stories, I would be happy to read it before you send it in.

I have a book recommendation for you: *The Sport of the Gods*. I know how much you love Paul Dunbar's poetry. It was written at the turn of the century but still worth reading. I would love to hear your thoughts on it.

I can usually manage a quick trip to Harlem on the weekends, but lately I haven't had a chance to get away. Unfortunately, it is not nearly as warm as friends tell me it has been in Harlem. There is nothing like spring in New York.

Respectfully,

Langston

April 9, 1928

I checked out a copy of Whitman's *Specimen Days*. Truth is, I was a bit leery about what a white man might have to say about soldiers from the Civil War. They did such horrible things to colored people back then. I couldn't imagine having to read about it. Back in Georgia there were always reminders. Some white folks never got over losing the war and made it their business to remind the colored folk in town the South was still the South.

Whenever things were especially stirred up, my grandmother would remark that it was still better than slavery days. She'd comb through the past for the most awful story she could remember about living on the plantation or working in the cookhouse. Mama would close her eyes and shake her head. After a while she'd say, *"Thank you, Jesus, there is a time to keep, and a time to cast away."* Grandma would agree and the conversation would change to something else. But images of my grandmother's stories would play through my mind for weeks. I still remember the story about the woman being beaten severely with a riding crop for burning the edges of the waffles. I'll never understand why the white women didn't do more to help the colored women.

Oddly enough, the notes in *Specimen Days* made my heart ache for the soldiers, Confederate and Union alike. So many lives lost. But I guess I should be grateful. Otherwise, I'd be on a plantation working in a cookhouse. Or I guess it would be a kitchen now.

April 11, 1928

I tried to write field notes when I got home from work, but to be honest, I couldn't think of anything worth writing about. Whitman's interactions with soldiers were certainly more interesting than people coming and going through the library. How can making notes about an ordinary day help me write?

April 12, 1928
Field Note – Observation

I sat down on the davenport to read but got distracted by the sag in the cushion, the foam finally giving way to years of Earl's afternoon naps and Junior flopping on it. It used to be we sat straight-backed to read or to receive guests. The children weren't even allowed to sit on it except in their Sunday clothes while they waited for Earl and me. Now, someone sprawls across the davenport daily as if it were a mattress. The whole room shows signs of age. The yellowed curtains. White threads bleeding through the pattern of roses in the rug. The lace shawl draped over the back of the davenport was the only thing of beauty in the room, even though it's older than everything else. I crocheted it while I was pregnant with Junior. Back when I used to wait for Earl to get home at night. I haven't crocheted anything in years. You only need so many shawls.

April 13, 1928

I wanted to try another field note today, but I stopped at the soda shop on 139th and Lenox after work to meet Agnes. She rides my nerves, but our afternoons at the soda shop remind me of when we were more like sisters than cousins. It was the only time I didn't feel like an orphan.

She had this brownish mark under her eye. I asked her about it, but she acted as if she had no idea what I was talking about. Something is definitely going on between her and Bud. Aunt Lucy probably knows, but I don't want to upset her by bringing it up.

Earl said it was probably nothing to worry about. Of course, that's his response to everything. It's too bad this can't be a field note. Some things shouldn't be written about.

April 15, 1928

I found an old copy of *Opportunity* in the hall closet at the bottom of a stack of magazines. Miss Hurston's story tied for second in their contest a few years ago. I hate to say it, but I didn't like the story very much. She made all the colored people sound so ignorant. There are people down South who talk that way, but she doesn't. Maybe there is more to it than I understand. I wish I could ask Langston, but it might offend him. They're friends. Truthfully, I liked the story she tied with, "The Typewriter," by Dorothy West much better.

It's foolish to think I could write as well as either one of them. It's a waste of time and paper. I'm not a real writer.

New York, New York
April 17, 1928

Dear Langston,

I loved your suggestion to observe my surroundings. I haven't noticed anything of value yet. The library may be magical because of all the books it houses, but the people are not as fascinating as you might think.

I checked out a copy of <u>The Sport of the Gods</u>. It broke my heart how quickly the Oakley family assumed the worse of Berry after twenty years of service. What reason would he suddenly have to steal from them? And why would it be so inconceivable that a colored man could save his own money? They think so little of us. And as soon as anything goes wrong, they blame it on somebody colored.

Back when I was about 12 years old, a man from my hometown was hanged for the murder of a white woman. Everyone believed her husband did it, but the authorities never even questioned him. It had to be the colored man. It makes me angry to even think about it. However, I don't agree with Dunbar that we are all at the whim of the gods. I couldn't help but wonder how a woman would tell the same story.

When I read stories written by men, I often find it difficult to empathize with the characters. Men never give the complete picture of women. For example, Dunbar only shows Fannie crying and being lost. But I'd imagine she was plenty angry at the Oakleys. At Berry. At the children. And even at herself. We don't see the struggle in her heart. She's limited to worrying about her daughter's reputation and the rent. Women think about a lot more than propriety and money. If more black women wrote novels, this would be clear. The women characters in Miss Fauset's <u>There Is Confusion</u> were as strong as the men.

I saw the writing contest in <u>Opportunity</u>. The deadline is awfully close. It would take me a long time to write a story worthy of publication. Even if

I could get something written, I couldn't compete with the caliber of writers who are frequently published in <u>Opportunity</u>. Perhaps next year.

I hope school is going well and that you had a lovely Easter. I enclosed a newspaper clipping on the Du Bois-Cullen wedding. It was quite an extravagant event. All of Harlem is still talking about it. I thought you might be interested since you know Dr. Du Bois personally.

Kindest regards,

Cora

April 18, 1928

I dreamt about the white man threatening my father with the horsewhip again. It's always the same. Me, crouched down behind the pickle barrel unable to move. The man with the whip raised over his head, yelling *I'm gonna kill you.* The crack of the whip. Mama screaming in the distance.

I woke up with a knot in the pit of my stomach. It resembles the way I would feel the mornings after one of those nights when Daddy came home late. We would pretend not to notice Mama's bruises, but the next day I would feel so jittery in my stomach I couldn't eat. For weeks after, my mind would replay the horrible things he said to her, the bangs against the wall and her screams.

I don't understand why the man is always white or why he is after my father. A colored man could be the husband of one of the women my father fooled around with. But I don't think he was stupid enough to fool with a white woman. A colored man could be lynched for even looking. It just doesn't make any sense. Mama and Daddy are long gone.

I bet Mrs. Jackson could help me figure it out. She interprets dreams for people in the building. But I don't know if I trust her enough to give her my hard-earned money.

Lincoln University
Pennsylvania
April 20, 1928

Dear Cora,

Thank you for the clip from the Du Bois-Cullen wedding. I left for Lincoln early Tuesday morning to get back to school. I did not have a chance to pick up a newspaper. What a spectacular event. Reporters from every paper you can think of. People — white, black — dressed in their finest, especially the ladies. The bridesmaids were charming and pretty in their pink dresses. I felt a little embarrassed in my rented tails, which looked more green than black. I hated to have to wear that dull, faded suit, but they were expecting me to be an usher. Nevertheless, green tails and all, I felt quite honored to escort Mrs. Du Bois to her seat before the wedding.

I couldn't agree with you more about The Sport of the Gods *being disheartening. Unfortunately, the story needed to be told. We cannot hide from the truth because it's unpleasant. Exposing it is the only way life will ever get better. I am finding the same thing is true with the survey I am working on for my sociology project. There are many people up here who don't want to look at the truth.*

I write because so many stories like Berry and Fannie's never get told. It is far better for black writers to tell the story. Take Nigger Heaven, *for example. Carl Van Vechten presented the problem of Negroes living in segregated and poverty-stricken Harlem. Most blacks were so troubled by the title; they never knew he handled the story with sympathy and humor. They distrusted a white man telling a Negro story. That's why you must push yourself to write something for the story contest. People want to read about black people. Not just other black people. The Negro is in vogue.*

Don't wait until all your other duties are completed to write in your notebook. Carry the notebook around. Jot down ideas, observations, conversations, and scenes as they happen. I grab whatever I can when a poem comes to mind. Much of my work has started on a napkin.

Lack of time isn't a valid excuse. There will always be something clamoring for your attention. Put the other things in your life on hold for a few months.

I have spent many hours talking to you over the years, and you are as intelligent and talented as any of the writers who have been published in <u>Opportunity</u>. The only difference is, they submit their work.

If you want to write, then write. You won't be any more prepared next year. <u>Carpe diem, quam minimum credula postero</u> — seize the day, trusting as little as possible in the future.

Respectfully,

Langston

P.S. Miss Fauset has a new novel coming out sometime this year. Nella Larsen's book, <u>Quicksand</u>, came out in February. Read it if you get a chance.

April 21, 1928

No one was home so I pulled the typewriter from the top of the closet. I sat at the kitchen table trying to block out the squeals of laughter floating in through the open window, and the stomping and cursing coming from the upstairs apartment. But the only thing that came to mind was how much I missed living in the country. It was hard to think with the crowded streets, crying babies, stomping feet overhead, and folks who don't know how to close a door without slamming it.

Finally, after about 15 minutes, I typed, "A strange man came to town," but then ripped the paper out of the typewriter, turned it over and started again. I could see the story in my head almost as if I were at the picture show — the man in a Model T driving down the main street of town and people on the street watching. But I couldn't figure out how to say what I wanted to say. Were the people on the street working in their yards or sitting on the porch? Did it matter? The story wasn't about them.

I was about to insert another piece of paper into the typewriter when Mrs. Davis called to invite me over to play pinochle. I shoved the typewriter back in the closet and tossed the paper in the wastepaper basket. Too bad I can't make a story out of what I write here.

April 25, 1928

I don't know what to make of Langston's last letter. The advice sounds reasonable, but he's a man. A young man at that. He doesn't have a husband or children. He doesn't understand what it means to work all day, then come home to take care of your family. I doubt he ever gets tired of people calling his name. *Cora, where is my shirt? Cora, have you seen my wallet? Mama, what's for dinner? Mama, can I have some money? Mama. Mama. Mama.* I can't take a bath without someone knocking on the door.

Tonight, instead of writing, I started the laundry. There was way too much to put off until Saturday. I used to do a little every night in the washtub in my kitchen until the landlord put a wringer washing machine with the attached motor in the basement. He charges 25 cents for the key. Earl says we should be saving those quarters, but he isn't the one rubbing the clothes on that washboard until his fingers are raw. That machine saves a lot of time, even though I don't like going down in the basement alone. It's damp and musty. The windows are so dirty you can't tell if it's day or night. And looking at those gray walls makes me feel like I'm in a jail cell.

I want to follow Langston's advice. After all, his work regularly appears in magazines, and he does have a published book of poems. I just don't know how to make more time to write when I have so many other things to do.

April 28, 1928

This probably doesn't count as a field note. I heard the phone ringing in the apartment on my way up from the basement. It stopped before I got inside. Then a few minutes later, it rang again. I barely said hello before Aunt Lucy insisted I come to Agnes's apartment immediately. She sounded as if she was crying but wouldn't tell me what was wrong. I grabbed my hat and pocketbook off the coat rack and rushed out the door.

The streets were full of people enjoying the sunshine. I had to weave through casual afternoon strollers and dodge peddlers for the entire two blocks between my apartment and Agnes's. A group of boys shooting dice blocked the entrance. I half expected to find Junior in the middle. I pushed past them, and I hurried up the four flights to Agnes's apartment.

Aunt Lucy stood in the doorway, waiting for me. Forehead furrowed. Lips pursed. Without a word, I went inside. Shards of glass peppered the floor, crunching under the soles of my shoes. I knew instantly what had happened. The overturned davenport. Lamps and tables scattered here and there. Splotches of blood on the wall.

"Where is she?" I asked, bending down to right a chair by the door.

"Resting," Aunt Lucy said.

"And Bud?"

"I don't know," Aunt Lucy said, closing the apartment door.

A shawl I had crocheted for Agnes years ago lay caught on the leg of the davenport with a large hole ripped in its center. I picked it up and held it to my chest.

Aunt Lucy stood by, silent.

"Is Agnes okay?" I asked.

She shook her head and fresh tears formed in her eyes.

"Let's go in the kitchen," I said, putting my arm around her and leading her out of the living room into the kitchen.

Aunt Lucy sat at the table, wiping her eyes with the corner of her apron. "Agnes brought the kids over to my house around 10:30 last night. Said she had to go find Bud."

I looked through the cabinets for their stash of liquor but couldn't find it. I sat at the table across from Aunt Lucy, taking her hand in mine.

"She ought to know better than to chase after a man when he's been drinking. If I've told Agnes once, I've told her a thousand times, don't fuss with that man. 'The wise woman builds her house, but the foolish pulls it down with her hands.'"

"Agnes is a grown woman," I said. But to be honest I was as worried as she was, maybe even more so. Despite the fact Agnes liked to pretend otherwise, I knew this was happening more frequently. Every time worse than the time before. He was going to end up killing her.

Aunt Lucy squeezed my hand and then pulled away. "I know, baby. I just hate to see her suffer so."

"I'll help you straighten up."

"I didn't call you over to clean up," she said.

"You want me to talk to Agnes?" I asked.

"No," she said. "I want you to go to the Fitzgeralds' house on Monday."

"Why?" I asked.

"To fill in for Agnes."

"Surely they will give her a day or two off," I said.

"She's going to need more than a few days and they will fire her. And that's the last thing she needs. I wouldn't ask you if I thought there was any other way."

She rattled on about what a good cook I was. How it would be easy. I told her I couldn't. I already had a job. All the while thinking, *I went to college so I wouldn't ever have to clean or cook for a living.* I was a librarian, not a cook.

"Cora, please," Aunt Lucy pleaded.

I sat in Agnes's tiny kitchen with my head buried in my hands. I wanted desperately to say no. But when I looked up, it wasn't Aunt Lucy

I saw. It was my mother. I nodded.

Aunt Lucy reached across the table and squeezed my hand. "Thank you, baby."

Before I left, I went in to see Agnes. Sunlight seeped in around the edges of the drawn curtains, casting enough light to see her swollen eye and busted lip. I sat on the edge of the bed. She flinched and moved away when I lightly touched her arm.

"I know what you're going to say," she said.

Though I knew my voice betrayed me, I told her I just stopped in to see how she was doing.

"It wasn't his fault," she said.

"It was," I said before I could catch myself.

"I shouldn't have pushed him."

I wondered if she meant physically but decided that it didn't matter.

"I should have let him go," she said.

I agreed with her, though I didn't say anything. Instead, I told her not to worry. I would fill in for her while she got better. She reached for my hand and gently squeezed it.

I left the apartment exhausted and angry. At Bud. At Agnes. At Aunt Lucy. I explained the whole thing to Earl. He said Agnes put herself in that situation and it wasn't my responsibility to help her keep her job. She should know better than chasing after some lowlife nigger like Bud. I wanted to argue the point, but he was right.

April 29, 1928

This morning when I woke up, it occurred to me that there had to be some woman at church looking for work. So, after service, I asked around. One woman was available but only on Wednesdays and Fridays. Another woman asked too many questions.

After supper, I called Mrs. Rose at home and requested time off to care for a sick relative. She told me to take as long as I needed. I complained to Earl, but he barely looked up from the newspaper. His eyes lost their luster like they do when he isn't interested in the conversation.

"If the money is the same, what difference does it make?" he asked.

"It would make a difference to you if you had to drive a white man around all day," I said.

"I would never put myself in that situation," he said with that smirk he gets when he thinks he's superior to everyone.

I came back here to our room and slammed the door. What have I gotten myself into?

New York, New York

April 29, 1928

Dear Langston,

I'm glad you enjoyed the article. I didn't realize you were at the wedding. The whole black literary community was there, even Mrs. Rose. I'd read so much about the bridesmaids' luncheons, suppers and bridge parties that I thought I might try for one of the public seats in the balcony of the church. But I didn't want to fight the crowd. I would have never thought people would line up four hours before the service to get in. The paper said there were three thousand at the church. I imagine it was much nicer to have one of those embossed invitations.

Thank you for the advice about jotting ideas as things happen. Unfortunately, it isn't as easy to do when you have a family. They are my responsibility, not a distraction. It would be wrong to push them away while I try to figure out what I want to write about. It might be different if I had a specific story to tell. But I don't. So, I will have to be satisfied with writing in my journal, especially now that I must help my cousin. She is not well, and my aunt has asked me to fill in at her job for a while. The whole thing would make an interesting story. Educated woman turns domestic.

Good luck with the last few weeks of school.

Sincerely,

Cora

April 30, 1928

Today I worked at the Fitzgeralds'. When I got home tonight, I dropped my bags on the davenport and headed to the kitchen to cook supper. Earl and Dorothy were sitting at the table playing checkers.

"We ate already. Aunt Lucy dropped off beef stew," Earl said without looking up from the board. I left the room, grateful he didn't ask how my day had gone.

My legs and back ached so badly. I wanted to go to bed, but the smell of the Fitzgeralds' supper mixed with sweat clung to my body. I stripped off my clothes in the bathroom. I didn't want that odor in my bedroom all night.

I tried not to think about my day as I sank into the tub. The tension between my shoulders thawed like a piece of ice. The warm water and menthol from the Epsom salts worked like tiny fingers, massaging the bottom of my feet and the small of my back. I lay there near sleep. The day's events played over and over in my head — from standing at the bus stop to washing the supper dishes. I finally gave up and got out of the tub to write it all down.

When I arrived at the bus stop this morning and saw the line of colored women, looking like a platoon of soldiers in black poplin dresses, I knew I needed a uniform, though neither Aunt Lucy nor Agnes bothered to mention it. And when that red-haired young maid answered the door in a crisp white uniform and little hat, I felt even more unprepared. Her fussing just made it worse.

"You best be hurrying. They've been up since dawn," she said in a thick Irish accent. It took me a minute to realize she hadn't even looked at me, because when she did her pale, freckled face hardened. I couldn't tell if she was afraid or angry. "What are you doing here? You don't belong," she said.

I explained I needed to see Mrs. Fitzgerald.

"The Missus isn't expecting you."

I told her I was the new cook, though I don't know why I said that. She eyed me suspiciously and insisted she didn't know anything about a new cook.

"You may not, but Mrs. Fitzgerald does. You had better let her know I'm here, or we'll both be in a heap of trouble," I said.

She raked me over once again with her cold green eyes before she hurried from the room through a heavy wood swing door.

If it wasn't bad enough that I was standing in a strange kitchen, wearing a gray dress where the help clearly wore uniforms, there was a pot of coffee on the stove and a stack of dishes in the sink. The clink of heels against the floor echoed from the other side of the door. My heart hammered against my chest. The door swung open and a tall willowy woman in a violet dress rushed through. I expected to hear about my infractions but instead she extended her hand and introduced herself as Eleanor Fitzgerald. As we shook hands, she expressed concern for Agnes's health and offered to contact a doctor she knew in Harlem. I assured her that wouldn't be necessary. The lilt of her voice reminded me of a much younger woman, though she looked as if she was about my age. But you can never tell with white women.

I followed her down a narrow hallway to the pantry. A row of five fish-hook hangers lined the wall, with an apron hung on one and a black uniform on the other.

"Agnes keeps one uniform here in case the one she's wearing gets dirty. How fortunate you appear to be about her size," she said.

Agnes and I shared clothes as girls, but sharing a uniform seemed different. Exchanging one colored woman for another. Tomorrow I will be prepared.

I scrubbed the few stains out of the uniform once I finished my bath and hung it up. The darn thing should be dry enough to iron in the morning before I go back to the Fitzgeralds'. I hope Agnes convalesces quickly.

May 1, 1928

I arrived at the Fitzgeralds' by 6:30 today before the family came down. Made coffee and batter for hot cakes. The four boys rushed into the kitchen around 7:30. I worked quickly to get their breakfast on the table, though I found it difficult to think over their rambunctiousness. Even their mother's occasional, "Now, boys you are much too loud," made no difference.

Catherine, the Irish maid, never introduced herself to me. In fact, yesterday she barely looked my way. I only know her name because I heard Mrs. Fitzgerald say it.

Today she came into the kitchen and said, "They're only like this when the Mister is away."

Before I could respond she left the room.

Those four boys ate so many pancakes I had to make another bowl of batter. I think they might have spent the whole morning eating if Mrs. Fitzgerald hadn't sent them off to wash their faces. When the boys came back downstairs, she ushered them out the door for a morning walk.

The house was instantly quiet. I watched them walk down the walkway from the dining room window. Catherine stood by me.

"Agnes gets them on their way before nine o'clock. Some days she packs a picnic lunch for them to take along," she said.

"That's good to know. Thank you," I replied, even though I knew she wasn't actually trying to help me.

The stew Aunt Lucy made lasted another day. What am I going to do once it's gone? I don't want to look at food, much less cook. Hopefully, it will be a few more days. Although, I haven't heard from Agnes or Aunt Lucy. I'll stop by there tomorrow on my way home if I'm not too tired.

Lincoln University
Pennsylvania
May 1, 1928

Dear Cora,

    I didn't mean to suggest your family was a distraction. I have taken care of my mother and brother for many years. At times, it feels burdensome, but I know there is no one else to provide for them. However, we still must nurture our dreams despite our responsibilities. Please accept my sincere apology for offending you.

    I hope your cousin gets well soon. Does she work for such tyrants that they won't allow her to have a few days off for illness? I imagine it does leave you in quite a predicament. What of your job at the library? I am having difficulty picturing you in a white woman's kitchen cooking.

    Perhaps you will find standing in for your cousin will give you an occasion to write. When I lived in Washington, I worked in a wet wash laundry. I unloaded wagons and sorted bags of dirty clothes. I didn't much like the job. However, many afternoons I would prop a book on the sorting table and read as I worked. I wrote a great many poems during that period of my life. I felt a personal struggle in my soul and learned how to write more in the manner of the blues or spirituals.

    It might be a good idea to take your notebook with you. You may find time to write between preparing meals. Sounds to me as if you already have a theme. Writing about service work would give expression to hundreds of colored women who could never speak for themselves. I believe that would make an interesting and enlightening story. I certainly would like to read it.

    I know you have a lot of responsibility, but don't let duty stop you from being the writer you are meant to be.

Sincerely,

Langston

May 2, 1928

I brought a notebook today. It's easier to write at the Fitzgerald table. No distractions, except for the lilacs along the fence outside. My eyes keep drifting from the notebook to the window. I think it's because it's still hard to figure out what to write about.

The only observation I have is that Mrs. Fitzgerald puts a lot of fuss into the weekly menu. It's typed out and posted on a corkboard in the pantry. It includes how many people are dining and which table linen to use. There's an equally detailed grocery list, but that's Catherine's. I don't have to do both, like at home. But then the list adds preparation guidelines that ought to be common sense — cook the beans earlier in the day to make the Boston baked beans for supper. It's as if she doesn't think the cook has enough sense to figure out how to get the work done.

Mrs. Fitzgerald's appearance isn't so fastidious. The chiffon and lace tea dresses she wears suggest someone less formal, more carefree. The drop waist and loose bodice hang with such ease from her body unlike this stiff uniform. Whenever I reach for something over my head, it feels as if I'm going to rip the sleeve.

I'm starting to see Agnes in a new light. I never heard her complain once and this job is hard work. At least the kitchen has everything you could possibly need — a brand new icebox, six-burner stove, double oven, broiler and storage drawer. The entire mothers' board from church could make Founders' Day supper and never get in each other's way. I imagine Mrs. Fitzgerald hasn't ever used anything in here.

May 3, 1928

Yesterday's observation was darn right boring. I should have written about how the alternating indigo and yellow circles in the tiles remind me of the pattern of my days. A wheel going 'round and 'round. Every day the same thing, in the same order, in the same way. No variation. No change. Muddling the mind. Blurring time. Draining the soul.

Or maybe I should have written more about Eleanor Fitzgerald. Her sad smile puzzles me. I told Earl she looked like she needed a friend. He said if I'm not careful Agnes will be out of a job. He doesn't have to worry about that. I've had just about enough of day work. Besides, even if I worked for her, the two of us would never be friends.

This morning on the way here I ran into one of the Fitzgeralds' neighbors, a bald white man in a bathrobe and slippers. He glared at me from his porch. A dull pain throbbed in the pit of my stomach. I nodded and smiled anyway. Whenever I'm walking though the white part of town, I feel the same sort of nervousness you feel when you're walking in the woods at night by yourself. Every sound seems to be magnified and you don't know if it's just your imagination or if there really is something after you.

"Where do you think you're going?" he said. I told him I worked for the Fitzgeralds. He turned around, shaking his head.

"The Fitzgeralds and their niggers," he said before going back into his house.

It took almost an hour before I felt like myself again. Whenever a white person treats me less than human, I feel as if I've been beaten. Their hate makes my soul ache. And though I know I shouldn't care what they think of me, it infuriates me that my dark skin matters more than anything else about me. They don't care what type of person I am. They don't care that I am a woman. They don't care that I am a Christian. The only thing they see is the color of my skin.

It's foolish of me to want to be Eleanor Fitzgerald's friend. She would never see me as anything more than a cook. And just because you have a colored woman working in your house doesn't mean you want her sitting at your table for a cup of coffee.

Mr. Fitzgerald left on Monday for a business trip before I arrived. There is a photograph of him on the mantel in the parlor. He looks a bit like his wife. They both have long narrow faces, though his nose is shaped like the beak of a hawk. Hers is straight and thin. The sparkle in his eyes and crooked smile says he knows he's a handsome man. The menu calls for two adults. I suspect he'll be home this evening. I hope he isn't like the man next door.

New York, New York
May 3, 1928

Dear Langston,

I apologize if my last letter seemed terse. The whole thing with my cousin was pretty upsetting. I felt as if I was being pulled in so many different directions. But as you suggested in your letter, I have found more time to write than I anticipated. At the library, I concentrate on finding resources for patrons, but at the Fitzgeralds', I'm free to think about anything I choose. I sometimes have as much as an hour of uninterrupted time in the afternoon.

Unfortunately, there isn't much to say about domestic work other than it's long and tiring. I doubt that would make a very interesting story. I keep hoping something will happen to inspire a meaningful theme. The closest thing I have is a conversation with Mrs. Fitzgerald about men and women. It has me thinking, but I don't know how to turn those thoughts into prose. Perhaps I'm missing something.

Thank you so much for asking after my cousin. I can't say how she's doing. I haven't talked to her since last weekend. I imagine things are okay because I haven't heard anything. By the way, the tyrant in my cousin's life is her husband, not her employer. My aunt was afraid he would do more damage if Agnes lost her job.

I hope your finals are going well. Will you be returning to Harlem for the summer?

Your friend,

Cora

May 4, 1928

Yesterday while I was writing, I heard the boys in the yard. I leapt off the bench where I was sitting and banged my knee against the table. The boys ran through the kitchen without even stopping for a cookie. Mrs. Fitzgerald slid into the spot where I had been sitting.

"My word, it's hot today," she said, her face bronzed and glowing as if she had been sitting in the sun all day. I limped to the table with the pitcher of lemonade and glass. "You poor thing. You must be exhausted, standing in here working all day. Come sit down," she said.

I sat on the edge of the bench across from her. She sipped the lemonade, and then out of the blue she noted, "Agnes has never missed a single day of work."

I agreed it was unlike her, though to be honest, I didn't know much about Agnes's work ethic. "I guess this just got the best of her," I said.

"I don't mean to pry, but I've seen the bruises. What happened?" Mrs. Fitzgerald asked as she pulled the sleeve of her dress down, covering her wrist.

"It's not my place to say," I said, wondering why she had on long sleeves when it was so warm outside.

She nodded and glanced out the window. "I hate hiding behind propriety, pretending everything is all right. I wish I could help," she said.

"Agnes doesn't want help."

"I hate to see a member of our family suffer," Mrs. Fitzgerald replied.

I got up from the table to frost the cake on the counter, wondering how many other members of their family wore a uniform. She continued to make polite conversation while I frosted the cake. She asked me if I was married.

"Yes, ma'am," I said.

And then she said, "I don't believe men and women are meant to live together. We are much too different. Whenever Mr. Fitzgerald goes away, I breathe easier and feel freer. There isn't such fuss over everything. Do you ever feel that way?"

"Yes, ma'am. I do," I said, thinking about the end of the day after Earl leaves for work. For that hour or so I get to just be before getting everyone off to bed.

Mr. Fitzgerald didn't come home for supper. Oddly enough, Mrs. Fitzgerald seemed more troubled than relieved. I wanted to tell her I understood the disappointment of another supper alone with the children. But despite the comradery of our earlier conversation, I knew my place.

On my bus ride home, I envisioned a world without men, like Wednesday night women's choir rehearsal. High-pitched voices, all talking at once. Or like the women in my building gossiping and meddling. I don't think I would do very well in that world.

Although I will admit there is a sense of freedom that happens when the men are gone. Women probably jibber-jabber so much because men don't give them room to think, much less talk. The moment a man steps into the room, everything changes. I stumbled across a serial in a magazine by Charlotte Perkins Gilman about a society comprised entirely of women. I thought it was ridiculous at the time, so I didn't bother reading it. I'll stop at the library on my way home tomorrow and see if they have a copy of that magazine.

May 5, 1928

Mr. Fitzgerald was sitting at the kitchen table with a cup of coffee and the newspaper when I arrived this morning. I've never seen a cleaner looking man. His smooth face glistened like a spit-shined pair of patent leather shoes. It was as if he had never shaved a day in his life. He glanced up from his paper and nodded when I came into the kitchen. I quickly checked the menu. Good thing. His breakfast is different than the rest of the family: poached egg, dry toast and coffee.

I felt nervous having him in the kitchen while I cooked. I tried to be extra careful in case he was watching me. I snuck a quick peek over my shoulder a few times, but he wasn't paying me any attention. When I set the plate in front of him, he glanced down, studied the plate then nodded. He seemed pleasant enough, but for some odd reason I felt the jitters in my stomach.

Catherine came into the kitchen. I tried to thank her for making the coffee, but she glanced over to the table and then put her finger to her mouth and shook her head. I asked her about it later.

"We don't want to upset the Mister," she said, without any further explanation.

I didn't think I would get a chance to write today because everyone was behaving so oddly. The children were quiet and went straight to their rooms after breakfast. Catherine helped me clean the kitchen. When Mr. Fitzgerald left at noon to have lunch at his club, you could almost feel the house sigh with relief.

Mrs. Fitzgerald asked when Agnes would be back. I told her I wasn't sure if she'd be well enough to return on Monday. I stopped at Agnes's after work today to check on her and to pick up another uniform. I've washed the one I have so many times the fabric is beginning to fade.

Agnes's apartment had been put back together. The only sign that anything had happened was the missing cocktail table and lamp, and the cast around Agnes's wrist. She was still wearing her nightgown at 6:30 in the evening. She didn't ask about work, just plopped on the davenport and started talking about Bud. Apparently, he never came back home. I told her he'd be back, but she started to cry.

"He's staying with a woman down on Myrtle Avenue. What if he's in love with her?" she asked.

It would be better if he were, considering the bluish black bruises on her face.

"Then you'll just have to go on without him," I said.

"And do what?" she asked.

"If you two keep this up, someone is going to end up dead," I said.

"Now you sound like Mama," she said.

I went into her room to get her other uniforms out of the closet. I barely paid any attention to her as she explained all the reasons why Aunt Lucy and I were wrong about Bud. Three uniforms hung in the center of the rod. I stared at those stiff, starched dresses wondering why in God's name I had allowed myself to get in the middle of this mess. I snatched the dresses off the hangers and went back into the living room, intending to leave.

"You all don't know what it's like to really love a man," she said as I walked past her.

"Love doesn't have anything to do with this foolishness."

"You're just like Mama, believing in some ole down South sense of duty. More worried about what a man brings to the table than the bed. Stuff happens when you're passionate with a man."

I stopped just short of the door with her starched uniforms gripped in my hand, whipped around to look at her discolored face. "I'll take a sense of duty over bruises any day."

Agnes jumped up from the davenport and charged over to where I stood. "You think you have it so good. You have no idea what happens at that club. Mind your own marriage," she said.

I balled up the uniforms in my fist, ready to pitch them across the room. "Don't try to drag me or my marriage down in the dirt with you. I know exactly what happens at the club. Earl works a job to feed his family which is more than I can say about Bud," I said as I walked out of the apartment.

She shouted something at me, but I ignored her.

Unfortunately, there's some truth in what she said about down South sense of duty. I saw it in Mama. And Daddy wasn't much better. He barely said anything to her unless he was fussing. She went along with whatever he said or did, mumbling under her breath: "Submit yourselves as unto the Lord."

Moments after Mama died, I noticed a smile on her face. I could never decide if it was because she had seen Jesus or if she was happy to be free. The day she died was the first time I realized he loved her as he sat at the kitchen table with his head buried in his hands.

Truth is, I don't think marriage works without some sense of duty. There are some nights when I worry about the women and booze down at the club, but Earl then comes home and gathers me in his arms. Whatever oats he has to sow get sown in our bed.

It makes me sad we don't have as much time to spend together as we did when we first got married. I used to go to the club almost every night to watch him play. I'd be so tired the next day at work, but it didn't matter. The thrill of watching him perform carried me through. In the evening, he'd be waiting outside the library to walk me home. We'd lie in bed into the wee hours of the night, making love and planning for the future. Now all we talk about is the children and paying the bills. Hard to be passionate when you're worrying about those things.

May 6, 1928

After an entire week of day work, I can honestly say it wasn't as bad as I thought it would be. I almost enjoyed my time in the kitchen. I don't have to do things like splitting a chicken breast into six pieces so it lasts for at least two meals. There's more food than the Fitzgeralds could ever eat. Their dogs eat better than most of the people who live in my building.

So even though my legs ache and my hands are dry from washing so many dishes, I can't say I'm worse for the wear. My mind isn't full of call numbers, titles and reference materials. I'm not constantly asking people to stop talking. The Fitzgeralds' kitchen is so quiet most of the day I find myself thinking about all sorts of things: *What should we do about Junior? Why are Earl and I fussing so much when we are together? How are we ever going to save enough money to move out of that tiny apartment?* But most importantly, I had time to think about writing. So much so I've finally come up with a theme to write about — a woman's duty. Now if I can just figure out how to put my thoughts into words.

The Saturday routine at the Fitzgeralds' is very different. There are a lot of people in and out of the kitchen. Mrs. Fitzgerald sat at the kitchen table a good part of the morning planning the meals for next week and writing out a grocery list. Catherine went to the market and once she got back we worked together to put away the food. Then I prepared a roast and some potatoes for Sunday's supper. I also made fresh rolls and a chocolate cake. The oven was on all day. By the time I got back on the bus, my dress was damp with sweat.

I wanted to go to Rueben's Club with Earl last night, but I was tired after rushing to do my own grocery shopping and Sunday preparations.

May 7, 1928

This morning there was a note on the board not to make breakfast for Mr. Fitzgerald. I was relieved he wouldn't be sitting at the table while I cooked. The breakfast menu called for rolled oats, eggs and toast. Last week, I threw away a half pot of oatmeal. So, I made less than the recipe called for and added a little brown sugar and cinnamon. There are too many hungry people in the world to waste food. I don't care how much money you have.

Breakfast was on the table, and lunches were packed in a picnic basket on the counter when the family came downstairs. A young woman in her mid-twenties brought the boys to breakfast. She introduced herself simply as Jane. I didn't find out she was the nanny until Catherine complained about having to clean her room. She must be good at her job because the boys were better behaved. She had them out the door for their morning walk before 8:30. Mrs. Fitzgerald didn't make it to breakfast. She wasn't feeling well.

I got started on supper early so I could have time to write. Just as I was trimming the fat off the pork roast, I heard loud voices coming down the stairs.

"You are not to consort with those women anymore! I forbid it. Why do I have to tell you how to behave? A woman of your standing ought to think more of herself than to be a party to such foolishness."

I could hear Mrs. Fitzgerald's voice responding, but I couldn't make out what she was saying, even though they seemed to be standing in the dining room door. The walls were so thin I could almost hear them breathing. I wiped my hands on my apron and looked around the kitchen for something else to do. The garden seemed like the perfect escape. If anyone came in looking for me, they'd think I went outside to cut flowers for the table. But I worried rummaging through the drawers for the shears would make too much noise. So, I stood there.

"I cannot fathom how you thought I wouldn't find out," Mr. Fitzgerald proclaimed, his voice louder than before.

"I wasn't trying to hide it from you."

"Weren't you? Sneaking around town like a two-bit whore."

"Arthur, please. Don't be so vulgar. I joined a women's group as you told me."

"I meant the Daughters of the American Revolution or the Upper Eastside Garden Club. Not that group of jezebels."

"Standing up for your rights as a woman doesn't make you a jezebel."

"Do not provoke me, Eleanor."

"They are doing important work."

"It's a waste of your time and my money."

He paused; I suspect to let her speak. But she spoke too softly for me to hear what she was saying. Then there was a loud pound against the table.

"Enough. I don't want to hear another word. You are not to attend another meeting. Period. End of discussion." Mr. Fitzgerald's voice thundered through the house, followed by heavy footsteps and the slamming of a door.

I tried to go back to trimming the pork, but the rage in Mr. Fitzgerald's voice reminded me of Daddy. Whenever he sounded like that, we all knew the slightest little thing would set him off. We'd do our best to make ourselves invisible. So even though I knew I didn't have anything to do with the Fitzgeralds' fight, I was nervous. I wanted to get out of the house, but it was only eleven o'clock. Supper still needed to be cooked and served. As I seasoned the meat, I heard sniffling coming from the dining room. I tried to ignore it, but it made me sad to hear her cry. I grabbed a cloth and the furniture polish from the pantry and headed out to the dining room. Mrs. Fitzgerald sat at the head of the table, staring at the wall, dark circles under her eyes. I asked if she wanted some coffee. She looked startled to see me standing there.

"No, thank you, Cora," she said, sitting up straight and tugging the sleeve of her dress down over her forearm.

Whenever Earl storms out of the house after a disagreement, it seems as if all the emotion of our fight settles right in the pit of my stomach. My head aches so badly I can barely see straight. I don't know if I'm mad because I didn't get to say my piece, or worried that he was right, and I was wrong. I end up wishing someone else had been there to hear the whole thing, so she could tell me which one of us was right.

Men always think they are right. They believe women can't think for themselves. But most women I know are just as smart or smarter than their husbands. Of course, if you say that to some men, you run the risk of ending up like Agnes.

I wanted to say something to help Mrs. Fitzgerald, but instead I rubbed and rubbed the table.

"I hate it when he talks to me that way."

I didn't respond. I just kept rubbing the cloth across the grain of the table.

"I am not a child."

"They have to control everything," I said.

"And there isn't anything we can do about it."

"No, ma'am."

Mrs. Fitzgerald drew a deep breath and then lay her head down on the table. "How much more must I endure?" she asked.

Her shoulders quivered. I wanted to rub her back and offer her my handkerchief, but I still wasn't sure if she was talking to me. And getting too familiar could cost Agnes her job. But then Mrs. Fitzgerald sat up and looked at me.

"I'm tired of playing with the children at the park. I don't want to attend tea parties with those ninnies from the country club anymore. How many cucumber sandwiches must one woman eat? And that ridiculous garden club. I'd rather face a firing squad than have to sit through one of their meetings."

It was hard to sympathize with her if I'm honest. I scarcely get to see my children much less have time to play with them. Wednesday night choir rehearsal is the only time I get to talk to other women outside of work. And yet there was something familiar in what she was saying. Doing the same thing day in and day out can drag you down to the point where you feel as if you're drowning.

"Perhaps it would be better if I had a job," she said, pulling a handkerchief out from under the sleeve of her dress and dabbing her eyes.

"Jobs get tiresome, too."

"People are naturally more pleasant when they engage in worthy endeavors. Arthur is like a completely different person at the bank. More vibrant. Happier than he ever is at home. I want to contribute to the world. To pour myself into something that matters."

Her description of Mr. Fitzgerald reminds me of Earl when he puts on his tuxedo. He comes alive. There's a spring in his step, as if he can't wait to get to the club. I thought it was because he was a performer, but it has always been more than a job to him. He loves what he does.

"Arthur spends so much time at the office. It would be infinitely easier if he slept there," Mrs. Fitzgerald continued.

"I thought that way about my father when I was a girl. He'd stay at our family store until the wee hours of the night. My mother would be so angry, but it never stopped him. He believed as long as there was cash in the drawer it didn't matter when he came home."

"My mother didn't care what my father did as long as she maintained her spot on the society page. Losing status as the bank president's wife was more devasting to her than the death of her husband. Both she and Arthur would be much happier if I were more like her. But I just don't see any value in a house full of staff fussing over trivial things like silver tea sets and other useless trinkets. Truth is, I much prefer the simplicity of our cottage." She stopped talking and stared out the window. And then as if she was thinking out loud, she continued, "I want to be free from all of it. I am rather tired of being Mrs. Arthur Fitzgerald. I want to be Eleanor again. Just Eleanor. Do you ever feel like that?"

I shook my head. It would be nice if more people, especially white people, respected me or Earl enough to call me Mrs. Earl James. But to most I'm always just Cora, or Sister Cora or Miss Cora.

"Cora, I have something I want to show you," she said as she stood up. Mrs. Fitzgerald disappeared into the library down the hall. She came back in the room clutching a small book to her chest. She handed me a book by Kate Chopin called *The Awakening*.

"Mrs. Fitzgerald . . ."

She stopped me mid-sentence. "Please call me Eleanor. I want to be Eleanor."

I tried to read the book after Earl left for work, but I couldn't stop thinking about our conversation. She treats me more like a friend every day. It doesn't make sense. There is no question she is the lady of the house when she interacts with Catherine. I wonder how she treated Agnes.

May 8, 1928

I've been writing field notes for almost a month, and still don't have anything written for the contest. So today I am going to work on an idea I have for a story.

It's about a young girl named Pearl. I'm not sure where that name came from, but it seems to fit. She's 13 years old, the youngest child and the only girl. She's taller than her mother but looks like her father. Her skin is a deep mahogany color, and she has thick black hair. Her mother constantly reminds her to act like a lady.

Her mother's name is Sylvia, and she is 32 years old, short (about five feet). Maybe that isn't important. Well, anyway, her skin is a brownish red, like copper, and she has long black hair that she wears in two braids twisted together in a knot on the back of her head. Sylvia believes that the Bible holds the answer to all your worries. Her pies and cakes are known throughout the county.

Pearl's father is Ernest Buford and he's 38 years old. His skin is about the same color as Pearl's, but his hair is very wavy. I don't think that matters. I'll just keep the detail. Ernest is six feet tall with big forearms and a strong chest. He's very attentive to the women who come in the store and works late almost every night. Pearl has two brothers, but I don't know what to name them or how old they are.

Where do they live? Maybe a town like where I grew up in Georgia. I can picture the details more clearly. The house just outside of town. The chicken coop and vegetable garden behind the house. The general store they own where colored folks and a few poor whites shop. Ernest's mother opened the store right after slave times. Mr. Buford, the father of her children, let her use a building he had in town after his wife died. The store does a pretty good business. It has a wide front porch at the front, with three rocking chairs. A couple of old men, Mr. George and Mr. Henry, come to the store every morning, sometimes before Ernest gets there. They smoke their pipes and sip out of brown bags. Pearl likes to listen to their stories, but her mother has told her countless times it's not right to sit around listening to grown men talk. The whole family works at the store on the weekends and in the summer, except Sylvia. Why did she stop? Something happened at the store. What? Does it have anything to do with Ernest and the ladies? I'll figure that out later.

Pearl's brothers have freedom to come and go, but her mother keeps her close to home. She spends most days helping with household chores and listening to her mother tell stories. Recently, Pearl has noticed her mother grumbling to herself about something, but Pearl knows better than to ask her about it. But then a lady from church comes to visit. Or should it be a group of women? A sewing circle or something. Then one of the women could tell Sylvia about Ernest fooling around with a loose woman in town. Does Pearl overhear it? That's something to think about, but now I have to finish fixing supper.

I've been up reading *The Awakening*. Something about the heroine speaks to me, though it's hard to empathize with a rich white woman lounging at the beach, fretting about her unhappiness. It's a bit like Mrs. Fitzgerald, complaining about not being able to play with her children. Why did she think it was so important for me to read this book? If I were a character at the resort, I wouldn't have time to even look at the ocean. I'd be cooking their food or changing their linens.

I do love how Kate Chopin started the novel. It makes me wonder how to start my story. But it's hard when I don't even know what it's about. Or why Pearl is important to me. Writing about her reminds me of myself as a girl. What does a 13-year-old girl have to do with a woman's duty? It would make more sense to write about Sylvia.

Earl had a surprise waiting for me when I got home. He stopped by Millie's diner and bought me a piece of her famous pound cake. The children were jealous he only bought me a slice.

"Just a little something for my baby," he told them.

We all sat in the parlor and listened to an episode of *Amos 'n' Andy* on the radio after supper. I don't like the show. It makes us sound like fools: "'Splain dat to me," "Ain't dat sumpthin'," "I say dis heah's Amos." But Earl and the children enjoy it, so I sat there and listened. I even laughed a few times.

Before going to bed, Dorothy hugged me and said she would be glad when Agnes was well enough to go back to her job. She and Earl act as if I haven't been home every night for the last week and a half. But I guess I haven't paid much attention to them. Earl reminded me of that when I grabbed my book to read in bed. He took the book out of my hand, sat it on the night table, turned off the light and pulled me close. It was nice to have time alone with him.

Lincoln University
Pennsylvania
May 7, 1928

Dear Cora,

No need to apologize for your previous letter. The frenzy with your cousin reminds me of an incident that happened when I worked in this club in Paris called the Grand Duc.

This little French dancer started to behave spitefully toward clients when they refused to buy another bottle of champagne. Undoubtedly, she didn't feel well. She was going to have a child. After an unpleasant interchange with the owner, he ordered an attendant to eject her from the club. On the way out, she threw a bucket of ice on the owner and the attendant slapped her to the ground with one blow.

Florence, the entertainer, rose from her seat to defend the little dancer. She said, "Don't touch that woman. She's a woman and I'm a woman and can't nobody hit a woman any place I work." The dancer recovered and hurled another ice bucket into the air. A waiter grabbed her and Florence grabbed him. Then the manager went after Florence. The entire club turned into a brawl — one side for the women and the other for the men. I found a place in the kitchen away from all of it. It took the waiters and me nearly six hours to clean up the mess.

The bright side of working for your cousin is perhaps now you will be able to write something for the contest. I am much better at my art when there's difficulty in my life. When everything is going well, I'm too busy enjoying myself. Discomfort and pain make me more alert. My emotions feel tangible. I see the nuances in human interaction more clearly. I ask more questions. It seems as if that is happening to you also. I wouldn't worry about whether or not you're missing something. Give yourself time and eventually one persistent idea will force you to put pen to paper. When that happens all your notes will suddenly make sense.

Finals are going well. I am looking forward to focusing my attention on my writing for a while. I plan to stay on campus this summer to work on my novel. I am not sure if I will have a chance to visit Harlem.

Sincerely,

Langston

May 11, 1928

I finished *The Awakening* today at work. I couldn't put it down. It made me think about my own life. I often feel as if my thoughts and feelings don't matter. Earl makes the decisions. I go along with whatever he says even when I know he's wrong. That's the way it's supposed to be: "Submit to your husband, as to the Lord." But sometimes it makes me so angry. It's bad enough being beat down all the time because you're colored, but then if you are a colored woman, you get beat down at home, too. Seems like you're always submitting to somebody.

I shouldn't complain. Earl is better than most men I know. But it bothers me that we have always done whatever we can for him to live his dream, while I pretend I didn't have one. It's not that different than Mrs. Fitzgerald, or should I say Eleanor, wanting to contribute to the world. She and I are both compromising some part of who we are for the sake of our marriages — sort of like Agnes. I wonder what type of meeting she attended to make Mr. Fitzgerald so angry. Maybe she spent too much money. There's only one thing men are more protective of than their money.

That reminds me of the letter I got today from Langston. It troubled me. He never mentioned which side he was on during that brawl in Paris. It isn't right to hit a woman. You can't be neutral. Either you're for women or you're not. I don't know exactly what I'd do in that situation, but I certainly wouldn't stand idly by and let it happen. At least, not anymore.

I shouldn't fret about Langston's letter too much. He knows a lot about writing. He was correct about one idea forcing me to put my pen to paper. But it's not as easy as I thought it would be. Every time I think I've gotten one sentence right, I find something that makes me have to rewrite it. But nonetheless, I'm one step closer to entering the writing contest because I finally finished the story about Pearl's family. I pasted one copy here in my journal.

Woman Stuff
By Cora James

Pearl watched the knife in her mother's hand slice effortlessly underneath the skin of a peach, cutting so thinly there was barely any orange flesh attached.

"How did you learn to do that, Mama?" she asked as her mother sliced the skinless peaches into pieces.

"Just something I learned," her mother said, not looking up from the work in her hands.

Ordinarily, one good question would lead her mother into a bunch of stories about growing up in Mississippi. But today each question was met with a quick answer, and then silence. The only sound in the kitchen was the rustle of the breeze through the sheer curtains. Her mother's stories were the one thing she looked forward to. They helped to pass the time. Without them, cooking was repetitive and dull. Pearl shared this with her mother and was told any woman worth her salt has to know how to cook and run a household. But Pearl wasn't much interested in being a woman. Too much hard work. She wanted to be more like her brothers. They got to climb trees and go fishing regardless of how much work needed to be done.

The only thing that even slightly interested Pearl about being a woman was the talks they had around the table whenever the ladies from the church came over for Bible study and dessert. They would all lean into the center of the table while one of them talked. Pearl knew whatever they were saying had to be better than the stories Old Man Johnson told on the porch of the store, because her mother shooed her away if she caught her listening.

"Mama, can I stay for Bible study today? You always say time in the Good Book is time spent with the Lord," Pearl said.

Her mother looked up from the peach she was peeling and smiled. "When did you get so interested in the Bible?" she asked.

Pearl shrugged.

"You know what I think? I think you just want to hear what the ladies talk about."

Pearl tried to hide the smile creeping across her face.

"Just what I thought, using the Good Book to be nosy."

"But you said I need to learn how to be a woman," Pearl replied.

"You ain't got no business sitting around listening to a bunch of grown women talk about stuff. Now, hand me that bowl up there on the shelf so we can get these pies done before the ladies come," she said.

Pearl filled six glasses with iced tea and laid out napkins and forks on the table while her mother changed into a fresh dress. The ladies, dressed in fresh, crisp cotton dresses like the one Pearl's mother was wearing, started to arrive at 1:30. Pearl served each of them a slice of pie before taking one herself. She settled on the stool by the sink to eat it, but her mother sent her outside.

"Go on out under the oak tree. It's nice and cool down there," her mother said.

Pearl went out the back door and down the porch steps. But instead of heading down to the oak tree like her mother had instructed her, she sat on the side of the porch where her mother couldn't see from the window.

Sister Ruby said an opening prayer. And then Sister Inez read from Titus 2:3-4: "The aged women likewise, that they be in behavior as becometh holiness, not false accusers, not given to much wine, teachers of good things; That they may teach the young women to be sober, to love their husbands, to love their children." The chorus of amens floated through the open window.

Pearl's mother asked the ladies what their thoughts were on the verse. One woman, Pearl couldn't quite make out who it was, said: "I know it's in the word but I don't want no old woman who don't know how to take care of her own man telling me how to act with mine."

There were a bunch of voices speaking at once, and then the slow creak of the screen door. Pearl quickly turned away from the house and pretended to study the pie on her plate. How did her mother always know what she was doing even when she couldn't see her?

"I knows you were out here listening. Get from off this porch. Run on down to the store and see if your Daddy needs some help."

Pearl, relieved that she wasn't in more trouble, handed her mother her uneaten pie and called Rex, the family dog. As she headed toward the woods, she could feel her mother watching her, but she knew better than to look over her shoulder to check for sure. Once she heard the bang of the screen door against the doorframe, she slowed down. What was so bad about a woman taking care of a man that her mother chased her away from the house? Seemed if her mother wouldn't mind her hearing about how to cook and clean.

Old Man Johnson and Papa George were sitting on the rocking chairs half asleep. Pearl slipped past them without either of them noticing.

A woman in a blue dress stood at the counter as Pearl's father bagged her groceries. "That dress is mighty pretty," he said as he handed her the bag.

"This old rag," the woman said, waving him away.

"You make even a rag look like an evening gown," he said.

"Oh, thank you, Mr. Buford. I'll see you later," she said, smiling as she picked up her grocery bag.

The smell of honeysuckle lingered in the air as she hurried out the door. Pearl watched her walk down the steps of the porch. The frayed hem of her dress dragged the ground and her shoes were caked with red clay, even though it hadn't rained in several weeks. Pearl's mother would have tanned her hide if she came out of the house looking like that. "Even if a lady only has one dress, she never looks raggedy. You can always wash and mend your clothes," she'd say.

Pearl's father was helping another customer when she came in the store. She grabbed the Sears and Roebuck catalog off the desk and sat on the stool next to the register. Customers made it a point to talk to her, as if it might help with their bill. They respected her father, even the white folks, if you could say that white folks ever really respected a black man.

No one wanted to offend Jackson Buford, the richest white man in town. Pearl's father was his son, though neither one openly admitted it. In fact, Pearl's father called him Mr. Buford like everybody else in town. But you could tell Mr. Buford felt a surge of pride whenever he came into the store. Pearl once overheard him comment to another white man outside the store that Ernest wasn't like the others.

At five o'clock, Pearl's father closed the store. She helped him pull down the shades in the front of the store and then selected a few pieces of rock candy.

"Your mama is going to get you if you eat that before supper," her father said as he rubbed the top of her head.

"You aren't going to tell, are you Daddy?"

"Your secret is safe with me. Run on home to help your mama with supper."

Pearl gave her father a quick hug and headed out the door.

"Tell your mama not to wait for me."

She wasn't surprised. He often stayed at the store after closing. Pearl once asked her mother what he did at night. Her mother turned up her nose and said, "Some ole man stuff." Pearl had watched him closely all day. He swept the floors, refilled the coolers and organized the shelves. And when no one was in the store, he went back to his office to work on the books. There didn't seem to be anything left to do.

When Pearl got back to the house, Sister Ruby and her mother were standing out front. She ducked behind the oak tree so they couldn't see her. Their voices traveled across the yard.

"It ain't none of my business, but I'd want to know about my husband," Sister Ruby said, looking down on Pearl's mother. She was nearly a head taller and twice as wide.

"I don't want to hear it, Ruby," her mother said, hands firmly planted on her hips.

"Sylvia, folks are starting to talk."

"I don't pay no attention to what folks say. And if you want to be welcome in my house again, you better keep that nonsense to yourself."

"I just hates to see you get hurt," Sister Ruby said.

"I'm done listening to this foolishness," Pearl's mother said. She turned around and marched into the house, slamming the screen door behind her.

Sister Ruby stood there for a moment as if she was waiting for Pearl's mother to come back. Then she shook her head and walked away. Pearl waited until she was well down the road before she crossed the path to the house.

Pearl's mother didn't speak to her when she came in the kitchen. She just continued to mumble under her breath. Every few words were punctuated by the slamming of something on the counter. Pearl eased the plates out of the cabinet and quietly set the table.

During supper her brothers rambled on about the score of the baseball game. Pearl ate silently as she watched her mother, who barely touched her supper. She didn't even question the boys when they asked if they could go down to the church and listen to choir rehearsal. She just looked up and said:

"Pearl, go with them."

The four of them left the house together. Pearl didn't ask the boys where they were really going. She just whistled for Rex and headed toward the church. They were almost there, when Rex ran off after some animal. Pearl chased him through the woods, but he was too fast for her. She turned around to head back to the church but realized that she was closer to town. Her father would be heading home before too long, and they could walk together.

Pearl didn't announce herself when she got to the back door of the store. Her curiosity about ole man stuff got the best of her. She tiptoed up to the dust-covered back window and crouched down beneath it. Her father's hard breathing sounded as if he had just run from somewhere. Pearl started to stand up to see what was wrong, when she heard a woman repeating her father's name: "Oh, Ernest, Ernest."

Pearl rose up just enough to see over the windowsill. Her father's back was to her. The woman facing the window had her blue dress hiked up around her waist and her eyes were closed. Pearl watched for what felt like hours before she crumpled silently to the ground, drawing her knees to her body. Her chest tightened and for a moment it seemed as if she might vomit. Her father's breathing steadied. The last thing Pearl wanted was for him to know she was there.

Pearl crawled around the side of the building until she was sure no one could see her. She stood up and ran toward home. She was deep in the woods before she finally stopped, plopping onto a stump to catch her breath. The image of her father and the woman flashed through her mind again. If only she had listened to her mother and gone with her brothers. She wiped her face with the bottom of her dress, leaving streaks of sweat and tears.

Pearl's mother was on the back porch, scrubbing a pot, when she got back. She tried to dash past her into the house.

"Hold it, young lady," her mother said, without looking up from the pot.

"Ma'am," Pearl answered, her back to her mother.

"Where were you?"

"Um, looking for Rex."

Pearl's mother stopped scrubbing the pot. "He's been back here a couple of times looking for you. Turn around."

Pearl resisted the urge to wipe at her face.

"What you been crying about?" her mother asked, hands on her hips.

Pearl swiped at her cheek with the back of her hand. "Nothing."

"Girl, I don't have time to play no games with you. I know something done happened. Out with it."

Pearl never lied to her mother, even if it meant getting the switch. "Honest, Mama. Nothing happened. Can I just go inside?"

Her mother tossed the rag in the pot and walked over to Pearl. She turned Pearl this way and that, inspecting her dress and legs. "I know that something done happened to you. Tell me or I'll get me a switch."

Her father's loud rhythmic breathing echoed in Pearl's head. "The dog was chasing after something. I went looking for him."

Sylvia eyed Pearl trying to glean the truth, but then shook her head. "I can't stand a liar. Fetch me a switch."

The tears started before Pearl stepped off the porch, but not from fear of a beating. As she ripped the branch from the forsythia bush, she felt the first real pain of womanhood.

New York, New York
May 13, 1928

Dear Langston,

You will be happy to know that your advice was right on the mark. One persistent idea led to a short story. I am one step closer to entering that writing contest, after all. I hope you don't mind, but I included a copy of the story in this letter. I would be forever indebted to you if you read it.

I am glad to hear your finals are coming along well. The end of the semester was always the most difficult time for me as a student. I often felt as if my brain were going to explode if I had to remember one more bit of information. I much prefer reading one book at a time and savoring it. Speaking of which . . .

A few letters back, you mentioned Nella Larsen's book, <u>Quicksand</u>. I picked it up a while ago, but never got a chance to read it. Mrs. Fitzgerald gave me a book to read called <u>The Awakening</u>. Have you ever heard of it? It was written just before the turn of the century about the same time as the book by Dunbar. The author, Kate Chopin, provided the insight that I mentioned was missing in Dunbar's narrative. She revealed the challenges of being a wife and mother. I saw similarities to my own life. Unfortunately, the author didn't seem to believe society could change because it ended tragically. Read it if you have a chance.

I am sorry to hear you will not be returning to Harlem for the summer. But I am very happy to hear you plan to write a novel. What will it be about?

Respectfully,

Cora

May 14, 1928

Eleanor and the boys were fed and out of the house by 8:30 in the morning. Too bad Catherine wasn't downstairs to see since she is always so worried about what time they leave. It makes me so mad that she's always watching me. Running her fingers across the countertop when she thinks I'm not looking. Rearranging the pantry and then commenting on everything I cook. Yesterday, she made a remark about how Agnes cooks the potatoes longer so they aren't lumpy. I've had Agnes's mashed potatoes before. Not only are mine creamier, but they also have more flavor.

I sat down to write after I finished the breakfast dishes but felt guilty about having so much free time. So, when Catherine came downstairs, I offered to help her clean the upstairs bedrooms. She pursed her lips and turned up her nose.

"The Missus likes things done a certain way. I won't have you messing things up," she said, thrusting her chest out as she left the room. You would have thought she was the woman of the house.

Catherine thinks she knows so much. I could teach her a thing or two about how to keep a house. For instance, if she stopped rushing through making the beds and took a little extra time to fold the bottom of the flat sheet into neat corners, the bed linens wouldn't be such a mess in the morning. And the white clothes would be a lot brighter if she wasn't so stingy with the bleach. It's too bad she's more interested in keeping me in my place than being nice to me. Both of our jobs would be easier if we shared the load. When I lived with Aunt Lucy, it only took us a few hours on Saturday to wash, cook and clean. Agnes and I would do the laundry while Aunt Lucy cleaned the house. Then, all three of us would work on supper for Sunday. Agnes and I would get to talking and laughing so that it hardly felt like work, especially since Aunt Lucy wasn't as particular as Mama about how things were done.

It's not that I want to be Catherine's friend. I just hate that she thinks her white skin makes her superior. But she is no better off than I am. We both cook and clean so a wealthy woman doesn't have to. It doesn't matter that I'm black or that she's white.

Eleanor and I have a lot more in common than Catherine and I. Boy, wouldn't Catherine be surprised if she walked into the library and saw me in my real job. But that will never happen. She doesn't strike me as the type of person who reads.

When I got home tonight, Dorothy was sitting at the kitchen table doing her homework. Instead of rushing to fix supper, I sat down and watched her write a series of letters and numbers from her math book to her notebook. None of it made any sense to me. I never was one for math.

"You need me to move my stuff?" she asked, barely looking up from her book.

"No. I'm in no hurry to cook another supper," I said.

Dorothy stopped writing and looked up at me. "Mama, can I ask you something?"

"Sure."

"Why are you still working in that white woman's kitchen? Isn't Cousin Agnes well enough to take her job back?"

I glanced up at the calendar on the wall. It had been exactly two weeks since I started working for the Fitzgeralds. I had spent the morning reveling in how easy the job had become and hadn't thought once about why I was still doing it. Dorothy had asked me something I should have been asking myself, though I didn't like her meddling in grown folks' business. It wasn't her concern where I was working or how Agnes was healing. Eleven is far from being grown.

I opened my mouth to correct her, but then I noticed her eyes looked red as if she had been crying. Why was she so upset? "I suppose Agnes should be better by now. Although, the last time I saw her, it looked as if her arm was broken or something."

"Broken arms take a couple of months to heal, don't they?" she asked.

"Yeah, I guess so." I had been so angry with Agnes after our last conversation that I hadn't wanted to talk to her. But I probably should have asked Aunt Lucy about the cast.

Dorothy opened her mouth as if she was going to say something else, but she shook her head and went back to her homework. I sat there for a few minutes debating whether to ask her what was wrong. To be honest, I wasn't in the mood. Cooking a second supper was the worst part of my day. Whatever I cooked for my own family was never as appealing as the meal I'd made earlier in the day. Eleanor offered me the leftovers, but I wasn't going to feed my family their scraps. Not to mention the fact that Earl would blow his top if I served him supper from another man's table, white or otherwise. So every night I made another complete meal.

I was in the middle of browning flour for gravy when Dorothy asked, "Don't you miss your job at the library?"

"Of course, but I promised Aunt Lucy I'd help Agnes," I said, as I stirred the water into the browned flour.

"What's the use of an education if you still end up cooking or cleaning anyway?"

I stopped stirring my gravy and turned around. "Dorothy, first of all, this isn't any of your business. And you would do well to mind your place. I'm going to work for Agnes as long as she needs me to and that's that."

"Yes, ma'am. I know it's none of my business, but I heard Daddy say working in a white man's kitchen is no better than being a house nigger. I don't want people to think about you like that."

Colored people always criticize slaves as if they had a choice whether they worked in the fields or in the house. We all know it had nothing to do with what type of person they were on the inside. It was all about how dark their skin was. And here we are years later, still carrying the same old resentment toward each other because lighter colored slaves got to work in the house.

I'm sure some women in our building take great pleasure in seeing me in that stiff black uniform. They probably think it serves me right for not socializing with them. But pain pierced my chest as it occurred to me my husband was the person judging me. I took a deep breath and swallowed the thickness in my throat.

"Despite what your father may say or believe, people do what they have to do. There is no shame in that. Jobs are hard to come by for colored people. The Fitzgeralds are good people and don't treat anybody like a slave."

"I'm sorry, Mama, for being disrespectful," Dorothy said, tears brimming in her eyes.

I turned the fire down on the gravy and sat back at the table with her.

"Dorothy, don't cry. Some people feel better about themselves when they put others down. That's why it's best not to let what people think bother you. I don't want to work in that kitchen any more than you or your father want me to. Hopefully things will be back to normal soon."

But to be honest, I didn't believe my own words. How could I not worry about what my husband thought of me? Why would he say that about me? Didn't he understand that I could never say no to Aunt Lucy after all she's done for me?

Our talk seemed to set Dorothy's mind at ease. She went back to her homework and even started to hum after a while. But it took everything in me to hold back the tears. The smell of the food on the stove made my stomach quiver with nausea. I also had no desire to see Earl when he got up from his nap. So, I went for a walk after I finished cooking supper.

I headed to Agnes's apartment. After all, she was the reason I was in this mess in the first place, but I didn't feel like dealing with her either. I was too troubled by Earl's comments. What would have made him say that? I know he believes everyone has a specific role to play. He is the man of our house and he takes that role very seriously. To him my role is to be his wife in his kitchen, cooking his meals, keeping his house, and raising his children. But it makes me mad that his view of me is so limited. If it were up to him, I wouldn't even work at the library. He tolerates it because we need the money. He would like nothing more than for me to be at his beck and call all day. His opinion of me is based on his beliefs about women rather than who I am as a person. Not unlike how Catherine's beliefs about me are based on the color of my skin. It doesn't matter to either of them that there is so much more to me than my color or my sex.

Maybe Earl would feel more at ease if I told him about my writing. I could explain to him how I feel more alive and free working in the Fitzgerald kitchen than I've felt in my entire life. He might understand. He knows what it's like to need to express yourself artistically. I wonder what he would say about the story I wrote?

May 15, 1928

I spent time with Mr. Fitzgerald this morning. I've avoided him since last week by setting up his breakfast in the dining room before he comes downstairs. This morning he popped his head in the kitchen. He looked exactly like every banker I have ever seen — hair slicked back; thin gray pinstripe suit, white shirt, black tie; forehead as shiny as his wing tip shoes.

"There is someone in here," he said. "I was beginning to think we had a breakfast fairy."

"No, sir. I just thought you might enjoy your breakfast and morning paper away from the racket in the kitchen," I said.

"That was thoughtful of you. It's too bad you are only with us temporarily. We could use someone who thinks."

He meant it as a compliment, but I didn't take it that way. It would have really shocked him if he knew I moved him in there so I didn't have to be bothered with him.

"Thank you, sir," I said.

He headed out of the swing door, but then came back in. "Thank you for the peach preserves. How did you know they were my favorite?"

"I thought you might get tired of dry toast every day."

He nodded. "I do. I really do," he said. As he left the room, it seemed inconceivable that just last week he was the same man who was pounding on the table, yelling at his wife.

I reread "Woman Stuff" and don't like it very much. It seems childish or something. Maybe it should focus more on Sylvia. It would be fun to write about the women at the Bible study. I've heard enough foolish conversations at church to write several stories. But the truth is, writing about Sylvia makes me sad, whereas Pearl reminds me of the more carefree times of my childhood, nosing around asking questions that no one wanted to answer. Mama was always sending me outside when I got on her nerves. There weren't any girls my age near our house, so I would always take a book. I spent hours sitting under that old oak tree reading. Maybe Pearl should go back to the store because she forgot her book.

No, that's not going to make it better. The story should be about adults. After all, Pearl does discover some pretty adult things. But if I write about Sylvia, I will have to write more about how she worries about where her husband is and who he's with. Or how she doesn't trust anything he says because he lies so frequently to her. Then about all the people around town who know what's going on. It must be embarrassing. Maybe that's why Agnes is so ornery all the time. Everybody knows Bud runs around. I've seen the way people look at her. My poor mother didn't much like to leave the farm other than to go to church. I suspect she wouldn't have gone there either if she thought she could have avoided it.

No, I don't want to write about all of that. It reminds me too much of the arguments I heard in the middle of the night growing up. It feels too much like airing my family's dirty laundry. I'm pretty sure *Opportunity* magazine isn't looking for that type of story anyway. They seem to be more interested in stories about men.

Even though both writers who won a few years ago were women, they wrote about men. It seems strange to me that they didn't focus on the women in the story. It would have been interesting to read about why the daughter in "The Typewriter" decided to learn how to type. Did she sense her father's frustration with his life and want to do better for herself and her family? And what did the woman in "Spunk" think about her lover killing her husband? Both stories treated the women like props or the setting. But maybe Dorothy West and Zora Neale Hurston wanted to write about women but didn't because they wanted to have a chance to win. After all, even Langston's poem that won first place was about a man. Black men aren't the only ones who have the weary blues. It would probably be better if my story focused on Ernest, but that doesn't interest me at all. I've had about enough of men.

I keep thinking about Earl. Was he saying I was no better than a house nigger for working in a white man's kitchen? Why the sudden interest in the social standing of colored women? And who was he talking to? I should've asked Dorothy, but I didn't want her to know how much the whole thing upset me. That's too much to put on a child.

When Earl got home last night, he slid behind me in bed and rubbed my stomach. Every muscle in my body tensed up. How could he say that about me in one breath and want to touch me in the next? He asked me what was wrong, but I pretended to be asleep. I didn't trust myself to say anything. If I asked him the questions on my mind it would have started an argument. I didn't want to be up all night fighting with him and then drag myself to the Fitzgeralds' by 6:30. I tried to sleep, but I lay there awake anyway until 4:30, analyzing every conversation we've had over the last two weeks.

Fortunately, Catherine was out of the house most of the afternoon running errands. I dozed off almost burning the cake but caught it just in time. I cut off the scorched bottom and doubled up on the chocolate frosting between the layers. No one knew the difference, not even Catherine.

I completely wasted an afternoon. I could have spent those three hours writing. But unfortunately, I'm not inspired by the difficulties in my life like Langston. I just want to lie in my bed and cry. Maybe that's why there aren't as many women writers as men. Women carry so much. I wish I hadn't sent that story to Langston. He will most likely think it as bad as I do. Writing is a lot harder than I thought it would be.

May 16, 1928

Eleanor took the boys to an exhibit at the Metropolitan Museum of Art, and Catherine left to run some errands. Though to be honest, I don't believe her. Her cheeks were a little too rosy. And when I asked her what time she'd be back, she stammered over her words until she got frustrated and said:

"Don't you be thinking you can slack off because I'm not here to watch you."

"Oh, don't you worry," I said. "There's a project I've been itching to get at. This afternoon will give me just enough time before starting supper."

She must have thought I was referring to the pantry. She tossed out a few instructions on her way out the door, as if I didn't know the oldest canned foods go in the front so they get eaten first. I hadn't planned to organize the pantry, but I did. It took me about thirty minutes. Then I spent the next hour and a half staring out the window at the flowers in the yard. I knew I should've been writing, but I sat there thinking about how much I've always wanted a flower garden. The few pots that sit on the windowsill in my kitchen are just pitiful compared to a real garden with trees and birds and fresh air.

Back in Georgia we had plenty of room for a flower garden, but Mama thought it was a waste of time. Whenever I asked for flower seeds, she'd say: *You want to grow something, grow something we can eat.* But I didn't want to grow vegetables. I wanted flowers. Miss Velma, a white woman in town who loved Mama's pies, had the prettiest flowers all around her porch. She had four or five different colored rose bushes that coordinated beautifully with the other flowers in her yard. I loved visiting her house but hated going inside.

Miss Velma kept a canary in a huge brass birdcage that hung from a stand in her parlor. The cage door was always open. I swear that thing watched every move I made. I knew if we were left alone, he would come after me. Mama would scold me whenever I hesitated on the porch. *I done raised you better than that. Get in there and speak to Miss Velma. That bird ain't thinking about you.* I'd go in the house, but never trusted that canary. I don't much like birds because of it. But today I enjoyed watching the cardinals flit around the yard. The red feathers seemed more brilliant than I ever remember seeing in the past. They weren't at all like Miss Velma's canary. Their chirping sounded like a melody as they moved around like tiny dancers. I never heard the canary sing.

Funny, today I feel a little like that canary. There is only so much I can do or places I can go. What would life feel like to be a cardinal? That might be something I could write about for my next story. I still have time before Catherine and the Fitzgeralds get back.

Notes on Cardinals

No one wants to read about some birds flying around someone's yard. What if the woman in the story is looking out the window and thinking about her life? She's troubled. The colorful birds catch her attention and make her smile. Why is she troubled? Or is she unhappy. Is she bored? I know I would be if this was my house and the maid and cook did all the work. She has to have money. If she doesn't, she won't have time to sit around looking out the window. Are there black women who live like that? There has to be. I'm sure Mrs. W. E. B. Du Bois or Mrs. James Weldon Johnson don't stand over hot stoves cooking dinner nor do they clean their own houses. The brownstones in that part of Harlem are nearly as nice as the Fitzgeralds' house.

Maybe I won't say whether or not she's black. Maybe she could just be a woman. Can I do that? Although, Nella Larsen's *Quicksand* had a lot of rich colored people in it. Does the main character have to be able to pass for white? There were plenty other colored people in the story who couldn't pass. So maybe it's not important. The characters in Miss Fauset's book, *There Is Confusion*, were all colored, except the one guy who was half-white. But Miss Fauset writes a lot about racism. I don't want to deal with that in my story. My character will be colored in my mind, but I won't mention it in the story.

Her name is Rose, and she's married, but I don't know what her husband does? Or if they have children? I'll leave that for now. If I fuss with too many of the other details I won't be able to start before Catherine comes back. I'm just going to start writing it in my journal.

Cardinal Story

A red cardinal sat on the fence. Its song floated through the open window. Rosie took a step closer to the window. Birds had always frightened her, even her grandmother's pet canary. She feared it would escape its ornate cage. But something about the cardinal made her want to study it. Her sudden movement spooked it and the bird flew away.

"I'd like to do that," Rosie said aloud, her voice sounding harsher than usual.

She waited at the window for it to come back, though she didn't quite know why.

A strange thing happened this afternoon at the Fitzgeralds' that I think might count as a field observation. I had started supper and settled into the alcove next to the window to work on the cardinal story. The words poured onto the page as if the pen had a mind of its own. I didn't hear Eleanor come in. When she called my name, I jumped.

"I didn't mean to frighten you," she said as she unpinned her hat and laid it on the table. I closed the notebook and slid it into my apron pocket.

"I hope you don't mind. I had some time while the roast was in the oven," I said, standing up.

"Of course not. So, you write!" she said, as if it were a shock that a black woman could write. "I have always wanted to keep a journal, but I haven't anything of interest to write about."

I opened the oven to check the meat. The room filled with the smell of baked onions and potatoes. The juices sizzled and popped against the edges of the pan. I had a spoonful up to my mouth when I realized Eleanor was watching me. She asked what I wrote about.

"People I grew up with back home," I said, pouring the spoon of juice over the roast instead.

"Memories?"

"Stories."

"Like the ones in *Vanity Fair*?" she asked.

"Nothing like that. Far from it," I said, though I suppose it isn't that far from it. A story is a story. But unfortunately, the editors haven't changed since back in the days when I wanted Mama to write down her stories for the *Ladies' Home Journal*. White editors still aren't interested in a colored woman's stories, because she is always going to be more colored than she will ever be a woman. They don't believe white women have anything in common with colored women.

I moved around the kitchen to look busy while we talked. She asked how I got interested in writing. I told her my mother took me to the library as a girl and I fell in love with books.

"Cora, come sit down," Eleanor said. "You're making me nervous, flitting around the kitchen."

I slid into the seat across from her. She leaned forward, her elbows propped on the table in front of her. Her green eyes were alert and bright, not like the day I found her in the dining room crying. "What did you think of *The Awakening*?" she asked.

The first thing that came to mind was how much I identified with Edna. But that felt much too personal to share, especially since I knew Eleanor was the type of person who always asked why. I didn't want to have to explain why I thought being married was the same whether you're colored or white. A woman is a woman. The only difference is a white woman has the luxury of her race and money.

"It made me think about how unfair life can be," I said.

"I know exactly what you mean. Men get to make their own choices. Why should a woman have to live a prescribed life because of her sex?" she asked.

Or a Negro because of the color of his or her skin, I thought. She went on about the roles and expectations society places on women.

I thought about the place in Genesis 3, where God says to the woman, "Your desire shall be for your husband, and he shall rule over you."

"God gave men dominion over women," I said.

Eleanor considered the idea, but then suggested it wasn't God's intention for women to be so unhappy. "Why would He have given women thoughts and ideas, if all He wanted us to do was service the men in our lives? We were made to experience life, too. To find contentment. Peace. Don't you want to experience life, Cora?"

"Where I come from women are supposed to find a husband and have children. Folks have a name for women who try to experience life. But men are supposed to get out and see the world. When my brother jumped on a cargo ship to Africa, my father practically threw a party to celebrate his independence. If I had done that, I wouldn't have been able to ever show my face in town again."

"But you came here. Isn't that your way of experiencing the world?"

"I didn't come here. My father sent me. He wanted me to get a good education."

Eleanor sat back, her eyes losing some of their earlier glimmer. "Many decisions have been made for me, too. I often wonder what my life would be like if I'd had a real say."

Earlier this morning I heard Mr. Fitzgerald scolding her like one of the children. He didn't like what she was wearing and instructed her to change before she left the house. "Spend that healthy allowance of yours on a decent dress, for God's sake," he said. For some reason it reminded me of how Bud talks to Agnes as if she is the stupidest person in the world.

I wanted to ask what she would have done differently, but that was prying. Besides, folks, especially white folks, are only going to tell you what they want you to know. There's plenty they don't want you to know, but the biggest secrets tend to be the most obvious.

"If I had more of Edna's resolve, I wouldn't be afraid to do what I want to do," she said.

"Edna ended up walking into the ocean," I said.

"I know. But if we are too afraid to step out of our comfortable lives, we risk dying, too," she said.

I wanted to laugh. I step on the trolley at 6 a.m. in order to make it to their house by 6:30 to make coffee. And before I worked at her house, I'd have to be at the library by 7:30. Comfortable is how I might describe my shoes, but never my life. "I'm not as worried about living as I am about surviving," I said.

Eleanor picked her hat up and tapped it lightly against the table. "Life can be so frustrating. But I refuse to accept that there is no hope. I want more. Don't you?"

I glanced around her spacious kitchen. Small puffs of steam seeped around the edges of the white enamel of the oven door. The copper faucet glistened as sunlight reflected off the hammered surface. How could I explain that if I had what I wanted I wouldn't feel envious of her porcelain cast iron sink with the attached drainboard? My house would be quiet during the day, but especially at night because I wouldn't live in a crowded building with more families than apartments. Or pay twice as much rent. Or worry about my son walking to the store even though, thank God, we don't live in the South. My husband would be able to play at Orchestra Hall with world-class musicians instead of Rueben's rundown nightclub. And I would be in my own kitchen, cooking my own supper.

"Of course," I said.

"What stops you?'" she asked.

My thoughts run through all the reasons why it's hard for Negroes to accomplish anything. But I could almost hear my father's voice saying that's just an excuse.

"I don't know," I said.

Eleanor nodded and stood up, the lines in her forehead visible for the first time. She picked up her hat and left the room. I sat there for a few minutes, replaying our conversation.

Even now, as I lay here unable to sleep, I wonder why I let myself run on so. It's so easy to talk to her. I forget that she's not my friend. Tomorrow, I'm going to keep my mouth shut no matter what she says.

May 17, 1928

Eleanor was extraordinarily quiet this morning. I feared it had something to do with our previous conversation, though she didn't seem angry with me. I decided not to push my luck by busying myself in the kitchen until she left for her walk. I was going to write more field notes but it makes more sense to work on my story. It needs a better opening scene.

Cardinal Story - new opening

A gentle breeze rippled through folds of the draperies, carrying a symphony of whistles.

"What-cheer, what-cheer. Tchip, tchip"

Rose glanced up at the tree outside the kitchen window. A cardinal sat perched on a low-hanging branch. Its bright red tail feathers flung over the side of the bough like the train of one of Rose's evening gowns. It seemed to be looking straight at her, as if it held the answer to a question she couldn't quite form.

Rose never cared much for birds. She feared the fluttering of their wings. It reminded her of the panic she felt whenever her grandmother's canary flew out of its ornate brass cage. She would beg for the door to be closed, but her grandmother would stretch out her finger to call for the bird

and proclaim everything deserved some freedom.
But flying around the parlor didn't give the bird
freedom. It always wound up back in its cage.
Freedom allows one to choose for oneself. The
thought troubled Rose. Was she any freer than
that canary?

I didn't get as much of my story done as I had hoped this afternoon.
It's almost as if I had written myself into a hole and I couldn't figure how
to get out of it. I thought it might help to get up and move around so I
pulled a bowl of fresh peaches out of the icebox and began to peel them
for a pie. The fuzzy skin on my fingertips calmed my mind. I've wanted
a peach pie ever since I wrote "Woman Stuff." I had Junior bring home
some peaches from Peterson's the other day, but when I cut into them, the
fruit was brown and mushy inside. The peaches Catherine bought were
perfect — not too hard, not too soft. The smell of cinnamon, nutmeg
and melted butter always brings a smile to my face. I was humming and
rolling out the crust when Eleanor came back in the kitchen.

She leaned down into the open pot of peaches on the stove and
inhaled. "That smells heavenly."

"My mother's recipe," I said.

"I marvel at how you and Agnes can just remember a recipe without a
cookery book. Whenever I cook, I need directions every step of the way."

"My mother drilled the details into my head. I don't think I could
forget them if I wanted to."

Eleanor leaned against the counter and watched me pinch the crust
into the bottom of the pie pan. "My mother never went anywhere near
the kitchen. The cook reported directly to our housekeeper," she said.

Well, that explained why Catherine was always telling me what to do.
I wouldn't last two days here if I had to report to her.

"When you talk about your mother, it makes me think growing up in
the South was different than I imagined. Can I read one of your stories?"

It felt as if Eleanor had asked me to pull up my dress and show her
my underclothes. "They still need a lot of work," I said, running my
fingertips along the edges of the folded sheets of paper in my apron
pocket. I had ripped the new story out of my notebook so it would be
easier to put away if someone surprised me again.

"I am sure they're better than you think," she said.

Something about her made me go against my better judgment. I reached into my apron pocket and handed her its contents.

"Thank you for trusting me," she said.

Once she left the kitchen, it took three tries to roll the crust to the right thickness. Mama would have been horrified to see the misshaped lattices I laid across the top of the pie. Eleanor didn't return until I was spreading the lace tablecloth over the dining room table for supper. She had my story pressed against her chest.

"It's wonderful," she breathed, coming over to my side of the table. "The way you started with the bird made me think about that yellow and green parrot in *The Awakening*. 'Allez vous-en! Allez vous-en! Sapristi!' Your words are so simple, but they make me feel the same sense of frustration."

I nervously fiddled with the tablecloth, smoothing out the edges I had wrinkled with my grip.

"I think you are as good as anything I've ever read in *Vanity Fair*," she said, as she rubbed my shoulder. The touch of her fingertips melted the fear frozen in my stomach. I wanted to reach up and hug her.

When I got home tonight, I hurried through supper so that I could work on my story some more, but Earl decided to take the night off. We sat on the davenport listening to the radio. Earl fell asleep about ten minutes into the show, giving me time to write before I went to bed.

May 18, 1928

I'm so angry I don't know what to do. Agnes called the Fitzgeralds this morning and asked Eleanor if she could come back to work tomorrow. I talked to Agnes last night and the only thing she talked about was how much she wanted Aunt Lucy and me to stop messing in her business. I told her nobody would be in her business if she had sense enough to leave Bud. She hung up the phone. Our whole conversation was typical. I didn't even mention it to Earl.

I felt like a fool when Eleanor came in the kitchen to talk to me. I pretended as if I had known all along, but I'm sure she could see right through me.

At least my family is happy. Dorothy said she was glad to have her mother back. But what she really meant is she's happy she doesn't have to cook supper anymore. Junior gave me a hug and said he liked it better when I worked at the library. It made him proud. Earl invited me to come down to the club with him to celebrate, but I was too tired and mad to be good company. I promised him I would go tomorrow.

May 20, 1928

Today Pastor Simmons preached on forgiveness. Well, it wasn't really as much about forgiveness as it was about being humble and long-suffering, which if you ask me is preached too much. If colored folks don't know anything else, they know how to be humble and long-suffering. But I didn't get annoyed until Pastor said, "Y'all come in here shouting and praising the Lord, but your hearts are hard as stone. Won't even speak to the person next to you, 'cause you mad. Don't want to forgive no body, 'cause they did you wrong. Want to hold on to your grudges, 'cause you got your feelings hurt. Christians in the pew, but sinners in the street."

It was as if he was talking directly to me, because if by chance Agnes had come to church this morning, I wouldn't have said a word to her. Fortunately, it wasn't Christmas or Easter, so there wasn't anything to worry about. Truth is, I didn't even want to talk to Aunt Lucy when she stopped me after service. She acted as if nothing had happened. But she knew I was upset. She gave me the same, sad bless-your-poor-little-heart smile she used to give me after Mama died. I know I'm not her daughter, but it still makes me feel bad when she favors Agnes over me. I should have known better. Whenever I get involved with Agnes's mess, I end up losing. I don't know what makes me madder — the fact she didn't have the decency to let me know she was coming back or the fact that she didn't even say thank you.

By the time we got home from church, I was in a foul mood. Earl asked me what was wrong, but I didn't feel like talking to him. Then he commented how glad he was to have things back to normal. I didn't respond. After supper, I went to lie down and unfortunately took the mail with me. There was a letter from Langston as well as one from my brother, Harold. I couldn't even think about Langston's letter once I read Harold's.

Their fifth child was born feet first, nearly killing his wife. Though it's been six weeks, Wilma is still too weak to get out of bed. And to make matters worse Wilma refuses to let any of the women from town help with the other children. She doesn't want strangers meddling in her house. Things had to be horrible for Harold if he is asking for help. I wish I could go down there to take care of Wilma and the kids, but I already told Mrs. Rose I would be back at work tomorrow. I'd look about as trifling as they come if I turned around to ask for more time off because of another relative. She'd have every right to fire me on the spot.

If he had written sooner, I could have spent the last three weeks in Georgia, helping my brother rather than fooling around with Agnes's mess. I only have myself to blame. If I thought more like Earl, I would have never put myself in that situation. What's done is done. Who would have thought that I would dread going back to the library?

Lincoln University
Pennsylvania
May 16, 1928

Dear Cora,

I read your short story. Nice job. I found the correlation between woman stuff and man stuff quite interesting, though what I don't quite understand is why you decided to make Pearl 13. Might it be more effective if she were older? Then we would be more aware of what she longs for. We know her mother broods over her husband's infidelity, but we don't know what type of woman Pearl wants to be. Does she reject the idea of womanhood? Or only her mother's? Or the woman in the blue dress? Miss Fauset's new novel addresses themes of womanhood. Too bad it hasn't come out yet. You might find it helpful to see how a colored woman writer handles the themes of societal expectations and identity.

I went to the local library for a copy of The Awakening, *but the librarian had never heard of it. Perhaps you can tell me more about it or maybe send me a copy.*

I have been thinking about my novel for a while. I'd prefer not to say too much about it. I still have a fair amount to sketch out. I will keep you posted on my progress.

Your friend,

Langston

May 23, 1928

I've had the worst headache the last three days. It started shortly after I got to work on Monday. I thought it might have been the weather. It's been so hot. Though the rain today cooled things off substantially, my headache remained. I took three packets of BC powder on Monday, but that didn't help. Tuesday, I went straight to bed after supper, but I couldn't seem to fall asleep. I thought I'd journal tonight rather than lying in bed looking at the ceiling.

I don't know why I've been so fretful. I should be happy to be back to my own life, but I'm not. The library doesn't feel the same. It seems darker and stuffier than I remember. And the women who work there are definitely cattier, especially Cynthia Goodman. It wouldn't surprise me one bit if she was responsible for me being vanquished to the back room, taping, binding and cleaning books like a first-year clerk. She has this look of satisfaction every time we cross paths. She still holds a grudge against me for being chosen as one of the hostesses for last year's Booklover's Club soiree. It isn't my fault that her tendency to only interact with wealthy or famous patrons backfired when she didn't recognize Langston. He came in one afternoon dressed as if he had been working at the docks. Cynthia wanted nothing to do with him. He and I started an easy conversation. I recommended one of his poems as something he might want to read, and he introduced himself to me. After that, whenever he came in, he made a point of stopping by the desk to chat with me. Our friendship was part of the reason Mrs. Rose asked me to be a hostess. She'd noticed the amiable manner with which I treat all our patrons, especially the writers. She told me she needed someone who was comfortable mingling with the crowd.

It's probably a good thing that I've been stuck in the back room. All week I've felt as if I were walking in a fog. There are so many thoughts going on in my head, but I can't seem to sort them out. The routine of my job has taxed me more than I expected, even though I haven't been as physically tired at the end of the day. It sounds strange to say, but I miss cooking. Though I suppose it really wasn't the cooking as much as it was the time I had between meals. Time to think and to write. I felt alive. Productive. Insightful. Like a real writer. And now it's over.

There's no way I'll have the energy to be creative after working at the library all day. The weekends won't be any better with all my chores and the noise in the building. Not to mention the fact that there isn't any space in this tiny apartment for my mind to wander or my thoughts to unwind.

It feels a bit like the discontent Edna felt in *The Awakening*. Something is missing from my life. Mere survival is not enough. I want more than a roof over my head and food on the table. I also don't want anger and bitterness etched on my face like so many women I know, including my own mother. She lived her whole life trying to be the virtuous woman described in Proverbs 31 — getting out of bed at the crack of dawn to make breakfast, baking pies to supplement the income of the store, mending our clothes so that we always looked well cared for, canning produce from the garden for the winter, ministering to the needy families in our community, and carrying herself with strength and dignity. And for what? She never earned the praise of her husband. Far from it. Only now would her children "arise and call her blessed." I love Earl and my children, but I want to accomplish more than taking care of them. Much like Dorothy, I once believed it was possible to have more. But somewhere along the way it became easier to accept that there's only so much a colored woman can do. But what I experienced in the Fitzgeralds' kitchen showed me there is more to life than trudging through the day.

Maybe I'm making too much of *The Awakening*. After all, Edna's quest ended in her death.

New York, New York
May 23, 1928

Dear Langston,

After rereading my story, I also concluded my decision to write from
Pearl's perspective wasn't wise. I considered rewriting it from Sylvia's point
of view, but I find her tiresome. It feels as if that particular story is Pearl's
and Pearl's alone. I do not know how to make it work better. Consequently,
I decided it would be easier to write a new story. I started one last week. I
believe it's more along the lines of what the contest judges are looking for.
Though to be honest, I'm not quite sure where it's going, but it feels truer to
the type of thing I want to write. Unfortunately, I won't have as much time
to write now that I have returned to the library.

I've enclosed Eleanor's copy of The Awakening. I'm certain she won't
mind as long as you return it when you are done. I recently finished reading
Miss Larsen's book, Quicksand. What an exceptional writer! She was quite
clever to use that stanza from your poem, "Cross," as an epigraph. It framed
the story perfectly. Miss Larsen describes things in such rich detail, it's
almost as if you are watching a picture show roll through your mind. It's
so exciting that we have so many eloquent Negro writers like yourself, Miss
Larsen and Miss Fauset. It will surely do wonders to change the perception
of the Negro race.

I am so anxious to know what you are working on. Are you sure you can't
give a hint?

Regards,

Cora

May 24, 1928

I've spent the last few days thinking about *Quicksand*. It was by far the best book I've ever read written by a colored woman, or man for that matter. But I wish Miss Larsen spent more time exploring Helga Crane's desire for individuality and beauty, rather than her struggle as a mulatto woman trying to figure out where she belongs. Then maybe the novel would have spoken more to the workings of a colored woman's mind. But most books written by colored authors are about race one way or another. And though I know it's important to talk about, I'm tired of that being the focus all the time. There are other things in life that are just as important. Dreams. Desires. But maybe that's too much to ask of a book.

I suppose that's the beauty of being white. Kate Chopin could write about the workings of Edna's mind and her personal desires because the color of her skin doesn't have anything to do with how she lives her life. I'm ashamed to admit I enjoyed the way in which Chopin explored the relationship between Edna and Robert. I wanted things to work out between them, even though I know it's wrong. I hoped their relationship would help Edna be more content with her life. That's why I thought it would have been more interesting if Miss Larsen had let Helga give in to her desire for Dr. Anderson, instead of always having her running away from him.

Truth be told, I miss the excitement of being pursued. I know Earl loves me, but I feel more like our old davenport. He looks forward to seeing me after a long day out of a need for comfort rather than real desire. Maybe Agnes was right. Maybe we have settled into some old sense of responsibility we learned from our parents. I guess there are worse things. Earl could be like Bud.

Mama used to warn me about thinking too much about the books I read. *If you want to ponder something, ponder the Word*, she'd say. I should have spent this evening reading my Bible or writing.

I tried to work on the story I started at the Fitzgeralds' but I don't know enough about Rose. It isn't like writing about Pearl or even Sylvia. They felt familiar. I guess it really doesn't matter. It's not like I would be able to finish in time to enter the contest. The summer is the library's busiest time.

May 25, 1928

I stopped at Lula's Beauty Parlor on my way home from work. Lula was sitting in the chair reading when I came in.

"Who died?" she asked, tossing the magazine in the stack next to the counter as she stood up.

"No one. I just felt like getting my hair done," I said as I hung my purse on the hook.

"Well, Miss Cora, come on over here and sit down."

I unpinned my hat and sat in her chair. She combed through my hair with her fingers and examined my scalp.

"Looks like it's done grow'd a bit since I last seen you. How about letting me use some of that hair refining cream? It works pretty good and lasts longer than pressing. Makes thick hair like yours easier to comb."

"I'm not sure I trust that stuff."

Lula sighed heavily and draped me with the cape. "I don't know how you manage this stuff on your own."

"It's not that bad," I said, though I often wished I could tie it up in a rag and not fuss with it at all.

As Lula massaged my scalp, working the shampoo into a lather, my neck and shoulders melted into the curve of the bowl. The tension of the last week probably would have gone away, too, if she hadn't asked me what was going on with Agnes and Bud. Apparently, the woman Bud was staying with came in the shop a few days ago, bragging about him leaving his wife. One customer called her a home-wrecking jezebel and another one asked how long she thought it would take before she had a broken arm and two black eyes just like Agnes.

"I tole her she can't come in my shop talking about taking another woman's husband. Especially a customer of mine. I hated to see that three dollars walk out the door, but this is a Christian business. I didn't allow that type of talk in my shop. God only knows why she or Agnes would want a man like that," she said.

"It's none of my business."

"Well truthfully, it ain't nobody's business, but it ain't right to beat on a woman like that. Somebody liable to wind up dead," she declared, wrapping the towel around my head and patting my back in a signal to sit up.

"Is your son still in Africa?" I asked, hoping to change the subject.

She spent the rest of the time I was in the chair telling me about all the places he had been and the things he had sent her. But I couldn't stop thinking about what she'd said. I planned to check on Agnes when I got home but forgot. Something didn't seem quite right with Junior. I could have sworn I smelled liquor on him, but when I asked Earl, he said he didn't smell anything. Everyone was in such a good mood. I didn't mention Junior's bloodshot eyes or the fact that he nodded off twice at the table.

I'm surprised Earl didn't notice, but men don't pay attention to little things like that. After supper I sat on the bed and talked to Earl while he got dressed for the club. The bounce in my hair made me want to put on something pretty and go with him. But something told me it wasn't a good idea to leave Junior alone.

To make matters worse, I had that dream again last night. This time my father wasn't in it, but I could see the white man's face more clearly. He looked a lot like Mr. Fitzgerald. Funny how the brain works. Anyway, I could hear someone crying in the distance, but it didn't sound like Mama. In fact, it didn't look like the store either. I've been lying here trying to convince myself that it doesn't mean anything. I should have gone to the club like I wanted to. Nothing like some jazz music to put your mind at ease.

May 26, 1928

I am going with Earl to the club tonight. I've had enough of sitting around the house moping over Agnes and the Fitzgeralds. It's just plain foolishness. Like Mama used to say, nothing but the devil's work comes from idle hands or, in my case, mind. Of course, she would have plenty to say about listening to the devil's music, but the way I see it, the nightclub is the lesser of two evils. And it beats the hell out of sitting around feeling sorry for myself.

Earl was so thrilled I was going with him tonight that he gave me some money to buy myself something pretty to wear. Dorothy and I went down to Myrtle's dress shop after we finished cleaning the house. I loved trying on all those pretty dresses and wanted to buy every one of them.

But I finally settled on a bronze silk dress with fringe along the hem. The fabric felt good against my skin — so different than the cotton dress I usually wear or that horrible stiff uniform I wore at the Fitzgeralds'. Dorothy and I both fell in love with the matching hat, but I'd already spent too much money. I might buy it in a few weeks when I have a little more money, though I have no idea where I'd wear it.

On the way back to the apartment I saw Junior walking down the street ahead of us. When I called his name, a man in a black pinstriped suit, walking a few steps ahead of Junior, turned around too. At first, I thought he stopped because he heard someone calling, but quickly realized that he and Junior were together.

"Junior! Where are you going?" I called down the street.

"I'll be right there, Mama." He turned back toward the man and said something. The man nodded and then tipped his gray fedora to me. As he turned to walk away, I realized it was the same man I had seen at Shorty's bar the afternoon I was out looking for Junior.

"Where were you going?" I asked again as Junior approached us.

"Nowhere."

"I'm going to ask you one more time," I said.

"Nowhere special, Mama. Just walking with Mr. Green."

"Mr. Green?"

"He's a friend of Mr. Peterson. We were just talking about fishing."

I glanced down the street. Mr. Green had already disappeared. And when I turned around again, Dorothy's narrowed eyes and pursed lips told me what I already suspected. Mr. Green and Junior were definitely up to no good. I didn't push the issue. Junior would just lie anyway. It was much better to let him think he pulled something over on me.

Dorothy talked the entire way home about my new dress and how to fix my hair. I could almost see Junior's mind working to figure a way to sneak out after we left. But as soon as I got in the house, I called Aunt Lucy to ask her if the children could stay at her house for the evening. There was no way he was sneaking out of her place. No one goes to the bathroom at night without her knowing.

May 27, 1928

I didn't make it to church this morning. My head hurt too bad to sit through all that singing and shouting today. I ought to be ashamed of drinking so much, but I'm not. It's sad to say, but I don't remember the last time I had so much fun. Though to be honest, when I first got to the club, I was in a foul mood.

Aunt Lucy met me at the door when I dropped the children off at her place. She wanted to talk to me. I should have told her I was in a hurry, but I didn't. Instead, I went in. She proceeded to complain that Agnes let Bud come back home. As usual, he promised her things would be different. I wanted to tell Aunt Lucy I didn't give a damn what happened between the two of them, but I sat there and listened for over an hour.

By the time I got to the club, it was packed with people. I've never seen so many beaded dresses and feather boas. Instead of sitting at a nice table and watching the show, I had to work my way through the crowd to even see the stage. The rumble of conversation made it difficult to hear the music. I tried to move closer, but this woman in a silver hat blew her cigarette smoke right in my face. It wasn't on purpose, but it made me pretty angry, nonetheless. I had a mind to head right out and go home. But then I found a spot next to a pole with a clear shot of Earl on the right side of the stage. He cradled the bass against his shoulder and his long thin fingers moved along the neck and belly, plucking the strings. I could feel the vibrations tingling down my spine. And when our eyes met, the gray haze of smoke and the commotion of people talking no longer bothered me. It was just me and him. I could have stood there all night.

I took the opportunity to look around the club during the piano solo. Earl always talks about different people from the club. I wanted to see if I could pick them out from his descriptions. Imagine my surprise when I saw Langston sitting at a table absorbed in conversation with a woman wearing the black boa around her neck. I must have been staring. He turned and looked straight at me. Then he came over to say hello. We exchanged pleasantries, and when the band stopped, he returned to his seat.

After the set, Earl joined me where I was standing. "Hey, I saw you talking to ole Slick there."

"We know each other from the library," I said.

"You're looking so good, I thought I'd have to come down off the stage and claim my woman," he said as he kissed my neck.

"He came over to speak, that's all."

"Yeah, well I know how he is. The ladies in here love him. Got a way with words if you know what I mean."

"He's a poet," I said.

"Yeah, I know. But if you ask me, sounds more like the blues. Just needs some music. Me and the cats in the band been trying to get him to put some words to the last tune we played. But he's been working on a book or something. I'm kind of surprised to see him here," Earl said.

"Me too," I said, though I regretted it. I'm not sure why.

"He used to hang out here all the time. Knock down a few drinks, shoot the bull with the band. Let's get some drinks."

We tried to make our way to the bar, but people — men and women — kept stopping Earl to talk. It wasn't until this woman in an orange dress stopped Earl and asked him to come over to meet her friends that I started to feel a bit uncomfortable. She plastered a smile on her face and limply shook my hand when he introduced me as his wife. She squeezed his forearm as we walked away. I asked him about it when we finally got to the bar.

"Ladies like to think they're special," he said as he handed me my drink.

I didn't say anything, but I could almost hear Agnes's voice: *You have no idea what happens at that club.* As we mingled with the crowd, I kept glancing over my shoulder at her. She quickly looked away when our eyes met. Earl must have seen me watching her because before he went back on stage, he kissed the edge of my shoulder and whispered in my ear: "Little-Miss-Too-Orange isn't my type."

The rest of the night I vacillated between watching Earl play and staring at the woman in the orange dress. Then my eyes would shift over to Langston interacting with the lady sitting next to him. It was like a scene from a picture show. The poet I occasionally write to, Earl, and Miss-Too-Orange — two perfect love triangles. It would make an interesting story. Maybe it could be about a man and woman who meet at the club and realize their attraction to one another. Now that sounds sort of fun.

A Cup of Coffee
By Cora James

Weary from the endless prattle of his companion, Everett glanced around the club for something to occupy his interest. That's when he saw Charlotte standing at the door. He recognized her in an instant. Her almond-shaped eyes and smooth, chestnut brown skin drew him in every time. He gave a slight nod, but Charlotte didn't notice. Her eyes darted from table to table, looking for someone. And before he had a chance to capture her attention, she turned away. He watched as she walked toward the dance floor, her bronze silk dress — so unlike the stiff, shapeless low-waist dresses she wore at the library — caressed her hips.

"Wouldn't that just be dreamy?" Mandy asked as she nestled closer, wrapping her arm around Everett's forearm. Her black feather boa brushed against his cheek.

He nodded in agreement, though he hadn't a clue what she was talking about.

"I knew you'd love the idea. You all should come along," she said to the rest of the table.

"I see an old friend," he said, as he pulled away.

Charlotte stood against a pole next to the dance floor, swaying in time with the music. The jasmine from her perfume wafted through the air like a summer breeze toward him. Everett leaned into her right ear and whispered, "Wanna dance?"

Charlotte stopped moving and turned slowly toward Everett, recognizing him immediately. A smile spread across her face.

"Hi," she said.

"Would you like to dance?" he asked again.

"I'd love to," Charlotte replied, sliding easily into his arms.

As they waltzed around the dance floor, Everett tried to think of something clever to say. But all he could think of was how the feel of her back against the tips of his fingers and the spice of her perfume made him want to descend deeper into the crevice of her neck. His heart pounded so rapidly against his chest that he wondered if she could feel it too.

"I'm surprised to see you here tonight," he said, hoping that talking would help him be less nervous.

"I like listening to the band," she said.

The music stopped and Everett reluctantly released her. Though he hoped for another chance to dance, the band announced their break. They stood there in the middle of the dance floor facing one another. Everett contemplated what to say. Should he ask if she was there with someone? What if she was? And what about his own companion?

He searched for somewhere to sit, but all the seats were taken — except the one next to Mandy, who thought they were on a date. But she wasn't his type. Mindless conversation and squeaky voices annoyed him.

"Would you like a drink?" he asked.

Charlotte glanced over her shoulders nervously before answering. "Sure," she said.

Everett wondered about the slight hesitation in Charlotte's voice as they walked to the bar. Surely if she were there for someone else, she would say something. Although, he hadn't mentioned Mandy, regardless of how he classified their relationship.

It surprised him at how keyed up he was around Charlotte. He normally had an ease with women. But as he looked down at the sparkle in her eyes, he knew she was different. For the last six months, she had been the reason for his frequent trips to the library. He enjoyed the ease of their conversations. He didn't have to be creative or clever. He wasn't a poet around her, just another person who loved the written word. They spent several afternoons poring over poems, discussing the poet's meaning and significance. Lately, he noticed something else simmered beneath the surface.

Everett handed Charlotte a scotch. And though he worried it would be too strong, she drank it easily. They silently stood next to one another, sipping their drinks as the band began to play.

"Let's go for a walk," he said, tossing a few dollars on the bar.

"It is rather loud in here," Charlotte replied.

Everett grabbed Charlotte's hand and led her out of Smitty's. Once in the cool night air, it occurred to him that he hadn't said goodbye to Mandy. He would definitely hear from their friend about that, but it didn't matter. He wanted to spend time with Charlotte outside of the library. They walked a block in silence, though his mind was brimming with questions.

"You didn't seem surprised to see me," he said finally.

"I knew you would be there."

Everett turned her words over in his head. Had she come there on purpose? "You knew I would be there?" he asked.

Charlotte nodded.

He stopped and faced her. "Were you looking for me?"

She didn't answer, casting her eyes down toward the sidewalk. He gently lifted her chin with his forefinger. "Were you looking for me?" he asked again.

"Yes," she said.

"Why?"

She frowned. "I had to talk to you."

Everett looked puzzled.

"I wasn't sure when you'd be back at the library."

"Sounds pretty important."

"Well, I bought this dress to come down here, but now I'm not sure what to say."

"You look lovely," he said.

Charlotte looked down again. "Please don't get the wrong impression. I just thought if we met out on the town it might be easier to get to know one another," she said softly.

Everett brushed a strand of hair away from her face and lifted her chin again. "You're braver than me. I've wanted to ask you out for a cup of coffee but was afraid you would turn me down."

"I'd never turn you down. You're my friend," Charlotte said.

Everett took her hand. "Would you join me for a cup of coffee?" he asked.

"I would be delighted."

They walked toward the flashing light in the diner window. Everett held her hand tightly in his, knowing that she would never be just his friend.

May 28, 1928

I finished another story in spite of constant interruptions. I settled at the kitchen table to write about Saturday night after Earl and I got out of bed. Around noon Aunt Lucy called to invite us to join her and the children for supper. I didn't want to go so I told her I had to check with Earl. Whenever she cooks a big supper, she invites everyone, including Agnes and Bud. I didn't feel like sharing a meal with them. Not to mention I loved the idea of having a free afternoon.

Writing in my own kitchen is so different than writing at the Fitzgeralds'. It's hard to stay focused. Earl kept calling me into the parlor to bring him a drink. And then he wanted to go back to bed since the children wouldn't be back until after supper. But I told him I had work to do for the library. I'm not sure why I didn't tell him I was writing. It's not like it's a secret. Maybe I was afraid he might ask to read it.

This time I wrote from the perspective of the man. I used the woman in the black boa sitting next to Langston as one of the characters. I had thought about writing about Earl and the orange dress, but it felt too similar to Pearl's story. Though it was easier to write, it felt as if something was missing. Charlotte seemed too much like the women in Dunbar's book. We don't even know anything about what's going on in her heart. All we know is that she wants Everett but we don't know why. I want to write something more like Chopin but about a colored woman. I don't even know if it's possible.

May 30, 1928

Today Mrs. Rose asked me to catalog the new shipment of books. Unpacking those boxes is one of my favorite jobs. It feels like Christmas morning. I can hardly wait to see what's inside. I love the crisp, woodsiness of the paper mixed with the pungent smell of ink. Something always jumps out at me riffling through the pages. I keep a pad of paper nearby to jot down the titles. It's a good thing Mrs. Rose made a rule that we can't check out brand new books, because I would have taken home volume four of The Hardy Boys, *The Missing Chums*. It took everything in me to not read the first chapter. I felt like my old self again. Writing,

Agnes and the Fitzgeralds were the furthest thing from my mind.

But when I came out of the backroom my heart nearly stopped. There was Eleanor, blank expression and hard-set mouth, solemnly engaged in a conversation with Cynthia. Her flowered silk dress and tightly woven cloche hat looked out of place against the worn pine circulation desk. Most of the women at the library, even the white ones, dressed more utilitarian. Their money and, for the most part, their time, focused on taking care of their families. I imagine Eleanor's dress cost more than most of them saw in a month.

Cynthia glanced knowingly over her shoulder at me when she realized I was standing behind her. Eleanor seemed to look right through me. Something sank inside. I immediately thought of that scene in *The Sport of Gods* where Mr. Oakley called Berry to his library to accuse him of stealing Francis's money. I could almost hear Catherine's Irish brogue claiming to have suspected me all along.

"Mrs. Fitzgerald would like to speak with you," Cynthia said, giving me a reproving once-over with her eyes. I acted as if Eleanor's request was completely natural, even expected.

"Thank you, Cynthia. Nice to see you again, Mrs. Fitzgerald," I said, forcing a smile.

"Is there somewhere we could speak privately?" she asked.

"Of course."

Cynthia, perched on a stool pretending to sort through a stack of books, watched as I led Eleanor to the reference table several feet away.

"Perhaps the reading room would be better," I said.

As we walked through the stacks, I tried to figure out what could possibly be wrong or missing. The family had nice things, but nothing of any value to me. If I wanted anything, it was Eleanor's freedom and lifestyle. And there certainly wasn't any way to steal that. Eleanor's formal mask fell off the moment the door closed. She looked more like the woman I chatted with at the kitchen table. The tension in my shoulders relaxed.

I gestured for Eleanor to sit and then sat across from her. "Is there something wrong?" I asked.

"Well, no. Not really. Though it is rather complicated. I suppose I should just get right to the particular matter I came to discuss."

The words "not really" and "complicated" echoed in my mind. I couldn't for the life of me figure out what she could possibly have to discuss with me. The muscles in my back tightened as if someone had pulled an invisible string between my shoulder blades. I shifted uneasily in my chair.

"Yes, ma'am," I said responsively, though it had been a while since I had referred to her that way.

She glanced down at the bag in her hand. Her look reminded me of that day I found her in the dining room crying. "It's been a long Fitzgerald family tradition to spend every other summer in Europe. For the last four years, the children and I have stayed behind. Jackson was barely two years old and before that Robert was too ill to travel. Now, Mother Fitzgerald believes the boys are falling behind in their studies because they haven't been exposed to classic civilizations. The boys are far too young to care about such things. Most likely, they will spend their time in the château with a nanny. Arthur has some banking business in France, so he will accompany his mother and the children. I will not be joining them."

As Eleanor talked, it seemed more and more unlikely she had come to chastise me. The tension in my back eased some. Though, I still wondered what any of that had to do with me.

She paused. "I have thought a great deal about your story over the last few weeks. I am astounded at what you were able to do in such a short period of time. I can only imagine what you could accomplish if you had the opportunity to focus on your writing. Why, your prose could be as good as any of the books I've ever read! You just need time to work on it without being bothered with a job. Even working at the library must get in the way of your ability to write."

More than you'd imagine, I thought.

"And since I have a summer entirely to myself, to do with as I please, I have decided to become your patron. I will give you a stipend for a few months so that you don't have to worry about working. And in three weeks, I would like you to join me at our family cottage in Upstate New York. It's perfect for writing. It's secluded and quiet. There won't be any distractions or responsibilities. All you will have to do is write."

As she continued to talk about how lovely the town was, I pictured a little desk with a typewriter overlooking a crystal-clear lake. I could almost hear the birds chirping in the background.

"I will be there," Eleanor continued, "but I won't get in your way. The two of us get on so well. I'm sure we'll make rather nice companions."

I began to think about how easy it would be to write if I had nothing else to do. I could go back to the story about Rose. Perhaps finish it in time for the short story contest at *Opportunity*. But then I remembered my husband and children weren't heading to Europe. I couldn't just disappear from my life for the summer.

"Eleanor, that is a very generous offer, but. . ." I started.

She reached across the table and patted my hand. "Cora, I believe in you. I want to help you."

"And I'm extremely grateful for that but the last three weeks at your house nearly cost me my job. I couldn't possibly take any more time off."

"Don't worry about that. I can make sure the library holds your job. Plus, I would pay you thirty dollars a week."

I thought of all the things we could do with the extra money. "I couldn't possibly leave my family for the summer," I said.

"Doesn't your husband travel with his band sometimes?" she asked.

"Yes, but never for an entire summer."

"It's only fair that you travel for your work?"

"Writing isn't my work," I said.

"But you want it to be. I'm offering you the opportunity to fulfill your dream."

"How would I explain it to my husband? He would never approve of me leaving for two months to fulfill a dream."

"We could tell him I need a cook for the summer. And if thirty dollars isn't enough, we will find an amount that is. If he's anything like Arthur, enough money will convince him."

"Won't Mr. Fitzgerald think that's a bit much for a cook?" I asked.

"He does not have to know," she said.

I tried to think of an excuse to say no, but I couldn't. I asked her for some time to think about it. She gave me a week.

When I returned to the circulation desk, Cynthia was busy with a patron. I grabbed a stack of books off the cart and headed to the stacks.

To be honest, it was hard to concentrate. All I could think about was Eleanor's offer and whether I should accept. Part of me really wanted to do it, but I couldn't figure out how to make it work. And then there were all the questions: What about Earl? Who would cook his supper? Wash his clothes? And the children? Who would look after them? If I weren't around, Junior would find all kinds of trouble to get into. And poor Dorothy would be home alone most nights while Earl worked and Junior ran the streets. And what about my job? Mrs. Rose would surely fire me on the spot if I asked for any more time off. But the image of me sitting at that little desk by the lake, pounding away on the typewriter kept coming back.

When I got home, Earl barely said two words before he left for work. Usually his moods upset me, but I welcomed the silence. I wasn't ready to talk to him about Eleanor's offer, though his opinion would be helpful. Men have a way of seeing things more clearly sometimes. They don't get all worked up about this or that. They just look at the facts and decide. He probably would know exactly how to make the whole thing work, especially considering how much we could use the extra money. On the other hand, he might tell me the whole thing was ridiculous. It might even make him angry. I wonder what other writers do in these situations.

New York, New York
May 30, 1928

Dear Langston,

I hope this letter isn't an interruption to your work this summer.
However, I need your advice. Eleanor has offered to be my patron. Have
you ever heard of anything like that before? The opportunity is more than
I could have ever imagined. And in spite of the many problems it creates,
I want to accept. Do you think I should? Is this acceptable in the literary
world? I would really appreciate a quick answer back. If I decide to go, I
have a lot to do in three short weeks.

Respectfully,

Cora

June 1, 1928

Last night after Earl left for work, Junior sat next to me on the davenport and asked me how I was doing.

"I'm fine," I said, not even looking up from the book I was reading.

"No, Mama. How are you?" he asked again.

"What do you mean?" I turned to face him.

"I don't know. You just seem tired." He ran his hand back and forth across the davenport cushion.

The truth is, I haven't slept very well the last few nights. I keep thinking about Eleanor's offer. Having an entire summer to focus on writing was a dream come true. And we could use the extra money. But then I think about Earl and the children. Who will mind Junior and Dorothy while I am away? What will Earl think about me leaving our family for a few months to chase a dream? Should I tell him the real reason Eleanor asked me to go? Or should I tell him I'm going to be their cook? He won't be happy either way. He probably won't let me go. Then I wonder why it is he has the power to let me go or not go. And then I decide I'm a grown woman. I can do whatever I want to do. He doesn't own me. But then I start to worry about the children. They need someone to look after them. If Agnes was a decent person, she could take care of them. But she scarcely looks after her own children.

"I have a lot on my mind." I patted Junior's hand.

"I know what you mean."

"What's on your mind?"

"Oh, stuff."

I felt a bit more suspicious of our conversation. "What kind of stuff?" I asked.

"Just school and whatnot," he said, as his eyes casually glanced from me to the clock on the mantel.

"Want some pie? I hid a few slices in the ice box," I stood up.

"You know me, Mama. I never turn down pie."

I sure do, that's why I know you're trying to butter me up for something, I thought to myself.

As we ate, Junior asked how I learned to make such good pies. I told him my mother and I used to make them for my father's store.

"Why don't you sell your pies?" he asked.

"Too much trouble."

"What trouble? You could do what you want, when you want."

"It's not that simple. I have bills to pay. I can't count on people wanting pies all the time."

"That's the trouble with colored people. They are always thinking about their bills rather than how they can make it," he said, shoving another forkful of pie in his mouth.

"Where did you hear that kind of talk?" I asked as I examined his face. He shot me a crooked smile.

"Around somewhere. I don't know, but it makes sense. You and Daddy are always worrying about this and that. There are a lot easier ways to make money than what y'all are doing."

"And how is that?" I asked carefully, so that he wouldn't stop talking.

"You gotta think on your feet. Like Mr. Green. Banks won't loan colored people money, so he does. They get the stuff they want. He makes money. He doesn't have to work for nobody and he never worries about his bills."

"How does he have enough money to loan to other people?"

"He has other businesses."

I knew something wasn't right when I saw Junior talking to that man a few weeks ago. He had hoodlum written all over him. I wanted to jump on Junior for hanging out with hooligans but figured it would be better to listen. So, I nodded and tried to act as if we were having a casual conversation.

"You seem to know a lot about his business," I said as I slid a piece of pie into my mouth.

Junior stopped chewing and looked up at me.

I smiled.

"No, not really. I just heard him talking to someone down at, um — Peterson's."

"I bet you hear all kinds of conversations down there."

"Yeah. I do."

"Well, you can't always believe everything you hear. Folks like to talk, especially when they think people are listening."

Junior bit the inside of his lip as he lightly tapped his finger on the plate.

"Well, anyway. Money's never been that important to me. I believe you have to do something that counts and at least something you're sort of good at, otherwise you're just marking time," I added, acting as if I were suddenly disinterested in the whole conversation.

Junior wiped his face and then stood up. "The pie was delicious, Mama."

"Thank you," I said.

He carried his plate to the sink and rinsed it off. "Is it all right if I go to the picture show with Lester and Henry to see *Lights of New York*?"

"What's that about?" I asked, even though I had seen posters about it on my way home from work.

"It's the new talking movie. I'm not sure exactly what's it about."

"Oh, that sounds interesting. Take Dorothy with you. She'd enjoy that."

The slump in his shoulders was visible from across the kitchen, but he nodded and left. I heard him trying to convince Dorothy to go. She finally agreed after he promised to buy her popcorn. I felt pretty proud of myself. Whatever he had planned wasn't going to happen with his sister in tow. I fell asleep before they got back. And for reasons unknown to me, I slept all night.

On my way to the bathroom this morning, I could hear Junior snoring in the back. I smiled to myself. Then the smell of whiskey and sweat hit my nostrils. I hadn't noticed it in our bedroom, so I figured it had to be coming from the open window. As I brushed my teeth, I thought about how much alcohol you had to drink for your neighbor to be able to smell it in their apartment. Then it hit me. The smell was coming from the back where Junior slept.

I found Junior sprawled across the top of his bed, still in his clothes. The smell of alcohol was so strong it made me gag. I whipped the towel in my hand across his back.

"Wake up!"

He didn't move or respond.

"Earl Junior, I'm talking to you."

"Huh?"

"Get up. You're drunk."

"I ain't drunk, Mama. I'm sleeping."

"Boy, get up this minute," I yelled.

He opened one eye. "Aw, Mama. Can't I sleep for a little while?"

Without even thinking I marched down the hall to our room, flung open the door and yelled for Earl to get up.

"Cora, it's too early for all of that yelling."

"Earl Jr. is passed out on his bed."

"Passed out?"

"He's drunk."

He picked the clock up off the nightstand. "How could he possibly be drunk at 6:15 in the morning?"

"I don't know how, but he is."

Earl sat up in bed. "Did he go out last night?"

"He and Dorothy went to see that new talking picture. I fell asleep before they got home."

He sighed. "So, you don't even know when he came home."

"Did you want to chastise me or see what's going on with your son?" I snapped back. Though I felt ashamed that I didn't wake up when they got home, his questions irritated me.

He mumbled something under his breath as he searched the floor for his pants. I regretted waking him up.

"I have to do everything," he said, pulling his tee shirt over his head.

I opened my mouth to respond, but quickly changed my mind when his deep-set eyes glared at me, daring me to say something. He pushed past me and rushed out of the room. I followed him. His heavy footsteps pounded against the wood floor, the vibration echoing in the walls.

"Boy, get your ass out of bed," Earl ordered.

Junior lifted his head and mouthed something unintelligible, then collapsed back against the pillow.

Earl kicked the foot of the bed and ordered Junior to get up. The fabric of his tee shirt stretched across his expanded back and shoulders as his body seemed to loom larger and larger. I stood in the doorway trying to think of something to say to defuse the situation. But the only thing that came to mind was how often I had chided Agnes about arguing with a drunk. What did I hope to gain by confronting Junior now?

Though we had only been standing there for a few minutes, Earl's anger seemed to multiply by the second, sucking the air from the room. I was torn between leaving and intervening. But just as I was about to suggest we let him sleep it off, Junior pulled himself up to a seated position.

"What the hell do you think you're doing, coming in my house drunk?" Earl asked.

Earl Jr. opened his mouth as if to respond, but his body heaved forward. A gush of vomit landed on Earl's bare foot.

"What the fuck!" Earl said, shoving Junior away from him and then bellowing for me to get something to "clean this shit up."

I turned to leave but thought better of it. "Go wash your feet and I'll take care of Junior."

"You woke me up because you couldn't handle it. I'm handling it now. Do what I told you to do."

"You're not going to talk to me like that."

"I'm not?" Earl asked, now standing right in front of me.

"No," I said as firmly as I could muster with my heart pounding rapidly against my chest. I knew better than to trifle with Earl when he was angry. But the instinct to protect Junior was stronger than any personal fear I felt. There was no telling what might happen if I left the room. So, despite the stench of alcohol and vomit permeating every breath, we stood there staring at each other for what seemed like an eternity.

"You get on my fucking nerves."

Earl pushed past me again as he left the room. The bathroom door slammed so hard against the frame that I heard the wood crack. But none of that bothered Junior. He had fallen back asleep.

The yelling woke Dorothy up. I asked her to make breakfast while I took care of the mess. Then I quickly got dressed for work, though I wanted to call in sick. I couldn't afford to miss any more time.

My head hurt all day long as I replayed the morning over and over again. It would have been better if I had waited to deal with Junior once I got home, especially since my conversation with Dorothy let me know what happened the night before. She told me they went to the picture show and came directly home afterward. He must have snuck out after she went to bed. I wonder if that Mr. Green has anything to do with it. Now that everything is stirred up, Junior will be on guard.

Fortunately, I found out what I needed to know when a friend from church came into the library. Her husband gambles a lot. We pray for him regularly at our prayer meetings. I asked her about Mr. Green, and she told me he is the neighborhood's most notorious numbers man and dope pusher. It's like Mama used to always say — *what's done in the dark always comes to light.*

I called home during my break to tell Earl what I'd found out but Dorothy said he had gone out. It was probably just as well. It takes him a while to get over being mad. She also told me Earl got Junior out of bed after I left for work, lectured him for an hour, and then made him clean the entire apartment. The call did a lot to ease my mind.

Something was burning on the stove when I got home. Without even taking my coat or hat off, I went to the kitchen to investigate. The water had boiled off the neck bones on the stove, scorching the ones at the bottom of the pot. Though I didn't much care for neck bones, I was relieved someone had already started supper. I added more water, then cut up the potatoes and carrots on the table. I threw them in the pot and turned down the flame.

I went to hang up my coat and hat but stopped to admire the newly waxed floor in the living room. Everything looked clean and bright, especially the windows. They almost glistened. I smiled to myself. I could spend Saturday afternoon at the museum with Dorothy instead of cleaning the house.

Earl was in the hallway, painting the doorframe, which had split when he slammed the door earlier.

"The house looks wonderful."

"There's neck bones on the stove," he said without turning around.

"I know. I turned them off. You must have gotten them from Mason's. Peterson's are always so fatty."

"I left some potatoes on the table. Cut them up and make some cornbread."

His instructions annoyed me. I managed just fine every single day without his help. But he was clearly still angry at me, so I didn't make an issue of his comment.

"You're not going to the club tonight?" I asked, unpinning my hat from my head.

"No," he said without any explanation.

I went back to the closet to hang up my hat and coat, all the while trying to remember the last time I took a day off work. Mad, sick, or otherwise, I went to work every single day. When I opened the closet door all the fussing in my head stopped. Everything that had been there this morning was gone, including the box with the old issue of *Opportunity* where I had hidden my stories.

"Where's all the stuff that was in here?" I asked as calmly as I could muster.

"I either threw it away or put it on the bed in our room for you to go through."

I quickly surveyed the parlor, hoping to find the magazines laid out on the table or stacked on the bookshelf. But they weren't there. Earl fussed in the background about all the papers and books around the house, but all I could think about was finding that box.

I ran back to our bedroom, hoping to find it there. The only thing I found was a heap of clothes and coats stacked on the bed. It would take half the night just to sift through what was what and clear it off. Though I was annoyed, I was still more focused on the box. Beads of sweat trickled down my temples as I walked back into the hallway. I tried to steady my voice before I spoke.

"There was a box of magazines in the front closet. Where is it?"

"In the garbage."

"Did you put it out there before or after garbage pickup?"

"How the hell should I know? If it wasn't out there when you came home, they picked it up. What difference does it make anyway? There's a whole damn library full of books and magazines. I don't see why you need to store so much stuff here. It doesn't do anything but clutter up this tiny-ass apartment."

Tears burned behind my eyelids. What was I thinking when I left my stories between pages of the issue with the contest guidelines? Now both were gone forever. All that work, writing and rewriting. And for what? All a waste of time. No stories. No contest. Nothing. A tremor rippled through my body. Earl turned and glared at me, the paintbrush still in his hand.

"That closet was a mess. And since the only way anything gets done around here is if I take care of it, I took care of it just like I took care of Junior today."

"Is that what this is about?" My voice cracked as the tears began to fall.

"Yep."

"What happened with Junior has nothing to do with you throwing away something that was very important to me."

"I don't want to talk about that damn box. It's gone. Get over it."

I didn't even know how to respond. I just stood there unable to speak or to stop the tears from flowing. It was as if I had just received news of someone's death.

Earl went back to painting the door but continued to fuss. "I shouldn't have to work all night and then take care of everything when I get home."

"You don't do everything. I work every day just like you. And then I come home, cook dinner, straighten up the house and take care of our children."

He stopped, eyebrows furrowed. "Take care of our children? If you had been taking care of the children, none of this would have happened."

"It's not my fault Junior got drunk."

"It *is* your fault. You should have kept better track of what they were doing last night."

His words hit like a blow to my gut. But despite his hateful tone, what pained me the most was the fact he had so little regard for what I did or the things that were important to me. It didn't matter that I worked as many hours as he did or that he had just thrown my dreams in the garbage. The only thing that mattered was I let my guard down by falling asleep last night. Now I was to blame for everything. My head spun as I imagined the pages of my stories strewn across New York's garbage dump. I wanted nothing more than to run out of the apartment, away from Earl, away from Junior, away from my entire life just like Edna —

"They were a part of (my) life. But they need not have thought that they could possess (me), body and soul."

"I've run all over Harlem trying to keep track of that boy while you sleep on the davenport or spend all night at the club."

"Don't start with me about the club. I don't want to hear that shit."

"Of course you don't. Maybe if you were around long enough in the evening you would know Junior's been hanging around with the numbers man."

Earl set the paint brush down in the bucket. "What numbers man?"

"Mr. Green. I saw him and Junior together last week."

Earl ran his hand over his head and then his shoulders slumped. "That's a problem," he said, his tone more concerned than angry.

"It is." I walked away to see about supper.

The potatoes and carrots were also scorched, but I didn't care. I scooped them into a serving dish and set them on the table. After Earl said grace, I excused myself. There was no way I was sitting through supper with him.

He came in the bedroom a little while later to let me know he was going out for a while. I just nodded. As I sorted through the things on the bed, it occurred to me the real problem today was that Junior got in the way of Earl's normal life. He was fine as long as he got to do what he wanted to do. And if I had thrown out his latest composition or anything that had to do with his music, he would never forgive me. Maybe it isn't fair since he doesn't know he did it. But I have no reason to believe he would act any differently had he known. The truth is, it's all my fault. If writing is so important to me, then I need to stop hiding it. Eleanor is giving me a chance to live my dream and still make money. There is no reason not to try.

Lincoln University
Pennsylvania
June 3, 1928

Dear Cora,

I apologize for not writing sooner. Though I've spent the last two weeks doing absolutely nothing, I did manage to take a trip to Harlem last weekend for one last wingding before starting work on my novel. But of course, you know that. By the way, it was swell to see you at Rueben's. I'm not sure why I never put two and two together when you talked about your husband being a musician. Earl and I have known each other for years. Too bad we all didn't get a chance to sit down and talk. Perhaps the next time I'm in town.

On to the question at hand — not only have I heard of writers having a patron, I have one myself. So do most of the Negro writers I know. It's the only way we can afford to write. My dear patron supports several of us. It was her idea that I spend the summer up at Lincoln working on my novel. She took care of everything. I can't tell you how freeing it is to not worry about money. When I have to work, it is as if the creativity is being sucked right out of me. I'd rather funnel my energy into words. Think about how much writing you got done when you worked in Eleanor's kitchen. Imagine the possibilities of having nothing but space and freedom.

I understand the hesitation of accepting money too easily from white folks. Far too often they are like Greeks bearing gifts. But you seem to admire and trust this woman. And it isn't like she doesn't have the resources.

You have to be willing to take a risk. Jobs will be there. There is always some place that needs someone to do something. And even if there isn't, no job will ever satisfy like following your dream. Accept her offer. You owe it to yourself and to the world. We need to hear your story.

I read <u>The Awakening</u>. *There were parts that reminded me of what you write about in your letters. I find it particularly interesting how some issues cut across race and class. But the black woman's struggle is compounded. She has to manage a racist society and the chauvinistic male. Though she may have dreams, they're stunted on two levels. I find that troubling, particularly as it relates to my novel. I hadn't given much thought to how my female characters felt about their role as women. I will have to give that some consideration. I will also need to think about their personal hopes and dreams, not just what's best for the family.*

All of this talk of the novel makes me realize I need to get to work. Be sure to write once you decide.

Yours truly,

Langston

June 4, 1928

Well, it's done. I telephoned Eleanor this afternoon and accepted her offer. Now I need to figure out how to make it work. I have to find someone to look after the children. Then I have to convince Earl it's a good idea. And then there's my job. Or maybe I should deal with the job first. If I don't figure that out, then the rest won't matter.

It's so unlike me to agree to something this big without having everything in order. But yesterday in church, Pastor reminded me sometimes we have to step out on faith before we see the way. I sure hope he's right.

June 6, 1928

Aunt Lucy stopped by for supper. I immediately knew something happened with Agnes when I saw the slump in her shoulders. I had Dorothy take the girls to her room to play while I finished making dinner.

"What's going on?" I asked as I poured her a cup of coffee.

"That chil' is gonna be the death of me."

"I thought Bud was back home and things were going to be *different*," I said, not brothering to hide my sarcasm.

"He ran off with that woman," she said.

I wasn't surprised considering what I had heard down at Lula's shop. "He'll be back," I said, as I pulled the dishes out of the cabinet for dinner.

"Agnes quit her job."

The muscles in my back tightened as a flush of heat traveled up my neck. "She quit?" I asked sharply.

"Yeah."

Three weeks of bus rides. Stiff uniforms. Cooking all day. Arguing with my husband. And she quits.

"She said she —"

"I don't give a damn. I've had enough of Agnes," I said slapping the dishes on the table harder than I intended.

"I know, Cora. It's frustrating but that's not all of it," she said, ignoring my comments and my anger. She went on to explain that not only had

Agnes quit her job, but she left the girls and followed Bud to Detroit. Aunt Lucy had no idea when or if she was coming back.

Fortunately, the conversation ended abruptly when Junior and Earl came in the kitchen looking for supper. Dorothy and the girls wandered in behind them. As I finished setting the table, Earl leaned close to my ear and asked what was wrong. I couldn't bring myself to tell him, at least not while I was still so mad myself.

After supper Earl took the children for a walk. Aunt Lucy stayed behind to help me wash the dishes. I was relieved she didn't say anything else about Agnes.

"I need to get away from Harlem. People everywhere. Peddlers. Garbage. Sometimes I feel like I'm going to throw up," she said as she dried the dish in her hand.

"I'd rather deal with the smells than Jim Crow," I said, thinking that the city was the least of her problems.

"Well, it ain't like you don't have to deal with that here, too. White folks in the North don't want to be around coloreds any more than white folks down there."

"Well, at least up here they aren't always reminding you of your place."

"I don't care nothing about that. I'm lonesome for home. I need to see trees and breathe fresh air."

The trees that line the streets of Harlem are almost like little orphans standing all alone. It makes me sad sometimes to look at them. It seems even the birds don't trust them enough to build their nests on the tiny branches. They are nothing like the tall trees back home with the squirrels running up and down the trunks and the hawks screeching from high branches. The woodsy area behind our house had so many trees that only patches of sunlight could break through the curtain of leaves on top.

"I'm sure some time in the country will make you feel a whole lot better," I said half-heartedly.

"It will. I'm even looking forward to the heat. The only thing that worries me is traveling with the girls. They can be a handful."

And then it hit me. Junior and Dorothy could go down to Georgia for the summer. At 11 and 13 they would be a lot of help to Aunt Lucy on the train. Then they could stay with my brother. Dorothy could help Wilma with the children and Junior could work on the farm with Harold. It would take care of the children for the summer as well as solve the problem of Junior and Green.

By the time Aunt Lucy left my mood had completely changed. Honestly, I wasn't all that surprised that Agnes left town. Or quit her job. It just annoyed me that I had allowed myself to be a party to her mess. Although, I guess if I hadn't, I wouldn't have met Eleanor.

June 8, 1928

Junior and Dorothy are getting on my last nerve trying to convince me not to send them to Georgia for the summer. Every conversation we have is about why they shouldn't go. Junior claims he's worried about his job at Peterson's. I told him if he's so worried, he should work harder at being on time. He didn't like that. Then he changed his tactic, questioning how we were going to make ends meet if he didn't make his contribution to the household finances. I assured him that we would be fine without his pay for a few months, especially since the money he gives me goes into a savings account for his future.

Dorothy tried to reason that the South wasn't safe. She shared the stories she heard from various neighbors about the way Southern whites treat colored people. I assured her there wouldn't be any problems as long as she and Junior minded their manners and did as they were told. But I also warned both of them that they had to watch what they said and how they acted around white folks in the South. Truth is, I almost changed my mind. I hate the way you always have to be on guard around whites there. But like Aunt Lucy said, it isn't much different up here. It's a fact of life. At least there is some comfort in knowing that Aunt Lucy and Harold will keep a good eye on them.

Anyway, once Dorothy realized her tactic wasn't working, she started to complain about all the fun she would miss over the summer. You would have thought she was a New York socialite. All the griping convinced me they both needed to spend some time out of the city. Besides, a little hard work and heat never hurt anyone. They will be better for the wear.

Now I need to figure out what to do about Earl. We're not angry with one another, but we haven't made up either. Maybe it would be better if I told him why I was so angry, but there's no need to bring that all up again, especially since he's not happy about the children going to Georgia with Aunt Lucy. At first, he said no. I explained that Wilma wasn't doing so well after having the last baby and how Harold really needed help with the other children. Earl said it wasn't our problem. He went on and on about how if my brother and his wife couldn't take care of their own damn children, they shouldn't have so many. That really set me off. I reminded him of how many times we have given his sister money to take care of her children. But that just made him mad.

"Send them money then, but don't subject Junior and Dorothy to two months of country-ass thinking and Jim Crow," he argued.

"I can send them some money, but then what do we do about Junior and Green? Do you have a better idea?"

He didn't respond. And it probably would have led to a bigger *discussion*, but he had to go to work. He never actually said the children could go, but he didn't say they couldn't go, either. I went ahead and made plans for them to leave with Aunt Lucy next week. I even talked to Mr. Peterson myself about Junior. Sad to say, he almost seemed relieved that Junior would be leaving for a while.

I'm supposed to leave in less than two weeks and still haven't told Earl about Eleanor's offer. It will be much easier once I figure out what to do about my job. I don't want Mrs. Rose to think I'm taking advantage of her kindness by asking for more time off. If only there was a way to make my absence a benefit for the library. Well, anyway, I better come up with something fast because I'm supposed to meet Eleanor for coffee tomorrow afternoon.

June 14, 1928

I leave for Upstate New York in two days. Even though everything has been worked out, I'm worried. Am I doing the right thing? I've never been so far away from family before. And what if there are no other colored people up there? Who am I going to talk to? What type of food will they have up there? I once heard someone at the library talking about white fish soaked in water, then covered in lye. I don't think I can eat anything like that. And who's going to cook?

Well, I guess that one is pretty easy. Eleanor and I are the only two people who will be there, so I will most likely be expected to cook. Catherine generally goes up a few weeks before the family to prepare for their arrival, but she took the summer off to visit her sister in Missouri. I don't know why it matters, but I doubt there's a sister in Missouri. Just like all those errands she used to run. I bet there's a man involved. Well, anyway I can't say that I'll miss those piercing green eyes, watching everything I do.

What will Eleanor and I talk about? I suppose I shouldn't worry too much about that. We conversed pretty easily last week when we had coffee. You would have thought we were old college chums. She told me about the spectacle her mother-in-law made boarding the ship and how happy she was that she was free from Mr. Fitzgerald and his mother for the summer. I wanted to tell her about the trouble between Earl and me, but it didn't seem quite right. Even though I call her Eleanor, she's still Mrs. Fitzgerald in my mind. I did, however, tell her I still didn't know how to get the time off from my job.

"It's too bad my absence can't be a benefit to the library in some way," I said, suddenly saddened by the reality that my trip wasn't going to happen.

"Why can't it?" she asked.

"I'm not sure what you mean."

"What if you weren't the one asking? What if I asked to borrow your services for a few months? Research or something like that. I'm sure they would be more than willing to give you as much time as you need."

"That might work, but that still doesn't take care of Earl."

Eleanor reached in her purse and handed me a hundred dollars. "I'm sure this will, if he's anything like Arthur."

I was reluctant to take the money, but I really wanted this to work out. So later that night I got the nerve up to tell Earl that Eleanor asked me to work at the family cottage for a month or so. I tried to be vague about what type of work so that I didn't have to lie. But he wouldn't leave it alone, so I told him that I would cook and help out around the house. I don't know why I didn't tell him the truth. It might have been easier. I wouldn't have had to listen to him lecture me about how there were plenty of white women in New York City looking for someone to sweat in their kitchens.

"You don't have to travel to some cabin Upstate to live out your crazy mammy fantasy."

"Maybe, but would they pay as well?" I asked as I laid the money Eleanor had given me on the table.

He ran his fingers across each bill as he counted it. Then he looked at me and shook his head. "I don't know what's going on with you and that white woman, but this is the last time."

I assured him it would be and he didn't say anything else about it. I thought everything was settled, but the next night he asked what he was supposed to do for supper every night with both me and Aunt Lucy gone for the summer. He also wanted to know who was going to keep the house and wash his clothes.

The question about supper was particularly aggravating. I don't know how many nights he has pecked me on the forehead on his way out the door and said, "Dinner looks fabulous, but I'll grab something at the club." But it wasn't worth arguing with him. Instead, I asked Mrs. Johnson from across the hall to share her supper with Earl while I was gone. She agreed because it hadn't been too long since I fed her husband for an entire winter while she went to Mississippi to look after her sick father. I offered to pay her when I got back, but she said that wasn't necessary.

To be honest, I didn't know what to do about Earl's laundry or the house. There really wasn't anybody to ask for help. So, I just left it. Earl was a resourceful man. He'd figure out something. But to be sure that it didn't cause any last-minute problems, I made all his favorites for dinner the other night. And then met him at the door after work in a lacy chemise and black stockings. It's amazing what a good meal and some time in the bed can do. He seems to be at peace with my trip. He even talked about the work he plans to get done over the summer.

I think it's a good sign that everything worked out. It must mean I am supposed to give writing a chance, although I'm not sure about all the half-truths and lies that I told to do it. I felt especially bad today at work when Mrs. Rose wished me well on my research trip. She was so proud of the 135 Street Library's contribution to Eleanor's project, though she failed to mention anything about the donation the library received. She did, however, lecture me on the integrity of the library and the value of this opportunity before I left.

"Not many colored women get a chance like this," she said.

I wanted to tell her she had no idea, but I simply thanked her.

New York, New York

June 15, 1928

Dear Langston,

I wanted to thank you for your advice about art patrons. I accepted
Eleanor's offer. I leave for Chesterfield County tomorrow. I'll be sure to write
to you and let you know how things are going once I get up there. I am so
anxious to spend my entire day writing. I have already written one story
and I am brimming with ideas for a few others. By the time August comes
around I'll have several stories to choose from.

Hope things are going well with your novel.

Fondly,

Cora

June 17, 1928 (Chesterfield County)

My, did the world change yesterday when I stepped on that train. Colors were brighter. The air crisper. Even my mind was keener. It's hard to believe I was so worried when Eleanor changed our plans Thursday night. We were supposed to leave Saturday morning, but she wanted to leave a day early on her own to take care of some business in town. The thought of traveling alone was terrifying. You never know how white folks are going to act. At least if I was with Eleanor, they would assume I was her servant and leave me alone.

I didn't say anything to Earl about the change in plans. Instead, I just lay there all night, worrying. What if they made me get off the train? How would I find my way to Eleanor's cottage?

Saturday morning, the commotion at the station reminded me of the train trip up North after Mama died. There were two lines — one for whites and one for coloreds. The porters helped the white folks with their bags, while the colored folks lined up in front of the colored-only car, bogged down with their personal belongings. I stood in line with my small satchel, thinking about Mama lying in the ground under all that dirt, trying not to cry. My father lectured me all the way from our house to the train station about the importance of hard work, but never explained why he was sending me away. He didn't hug me or even pat me on the back before sending me off to join the other colored folks boarding the train.

No one in line said a word or smiled, but there was a feeling of anticipation and maybe even relief. I looked over my shoulders to where my father was standing, hoping he would change his mind, but I couldn't find him anywhere on the platform. Tears clouded my vision as I stepped aboard and walked past rows of rough wood benches, searching for a place to sit. The only available spot was between two large women, one with a crying baby and one who smelled as if she hadn't bathed in a month. They each slid over to let me in. I could feel the heat from their bodies passing through my dress. The odor from under the one woman's arms laced every breath. Halfway through the trip she opened her oil-stained bag and began eating half a chicken. The smell of grease and sweat mixed together made me sick to my stomach.

Though I had felt more hopeful yesterday, walking along the platform alone frightened me. When a Pullman porter offered to take my bags, I didn't realize he was trying to help me. His smile put me at ease. It was as if he understood my confusion. He led me through a chestnut door into a cabin with 20 or so red velvet seats — nothing like the pine benches I remembered. As we passed through the aisle, a few white men dressed in suits frowned over the top of their newspapers, but no one said anything. My face must have shown my anxiety, because the porter leaned in close to my ear and whispered.

"No Jim Crow law on this train," he said. "Sit back and enjoy yourself. Ain't nobody going to bother you."

I settled into a seat by the window, marveling at the plush seats and running my fingers over the smooth thick fabric. My body nestled into the cushions. I couldn't have been more comfortable if I were sitting in someone's parlor.

Outside the window I noticed people tossing rice at a man and a woman as they boarded the train. The couple came through the chestnut doors and sat two rows in front of me. The woman did a double take when she saw me, but she quickly turned back to the people on the platform. She and her husband alternated between cooing at each other and waving to their family and friends. She wasn't a pretty woman. Her dull brown hair and angular face reminded me of Brontë's description of Jane Eyre. She did, however, have on the most beautiful yellow organdy dress. It made her look like an extension of the daisies on her wrist corsage.

Once the train pulled out of the station, the rumbling movement along tracks and the flash of scenery by the windows captured everyone's attention, including my own. With each trumpet-blast of the train's whistle I felt more relaxed. The rolling hills and dense trees reeled before my eyes like scenes from a picture show. I made up stories in my mind as we passed lone farmhouses and little white churches.

I might have spent the entire train ride that way if it weren't for another couple sitting directly across from me. They were traveling with three small children. The bewildered look on the woman's face suggested she wasn't used to managing the children without help. She tried to cajole the two older ones, who were climbing all over the seats, throwing things at one another. They weren't much interested in listening to her. The father never looked up from his book.

One of the men who had given me the evil eye earlier watched intently — visibly annoyed. The woman smiled weakly, but after a while he got up in disgust and left the car. I wanted to offer to help her, but I didn't think it was wise to intervene. I just sat there watching, feeling bad for the woman and everyone else in the cabin. Finally, the father tossed the book in the seat next to him and said, "For God's sake, Rebecca. You are disrupting the entire train."

She apologized to him softly, but he stood up and walked away. The father's departure must have frightened the children because they settled down moments after he left. And before long they fell asleep. Once the cabin was quiet, I noticed the mother's teary eyes. I wanted to offer her my handkerchief, but I knew from experience those were private tears. Some things are the same for women whether you're colored or white.

The whole scene reminded me of the short story I started before I left the Fitzgeralds'. I pulled out my notebook and began to sketch out more details about Rose. Her unhappiness seems related to the tears I saw in that woman's eyes, though it was difficult to put into words. As a woman, you never belong to yourself. You are either someone's daughter or wife or mother. And there's so much in the world hellbent on keeping you in your place. It doesn't matter what color you are or how much money you have. It feels as if there is no one else in the world who understands. How do you take all of that and make it into a story? Maybe Langston can help.

After a while, the train slowed down at a building about the size of the shed behind our house back in Georgia. My stomach twisted into a bundle of nerves when I realized I hadn't thought to ask Eleanor for the house number of the cottage or a telephone number where she could be reached. But before I had a chance to worry myself into a tizzy, I spotted Mr. Fitzgerald leaning against a black Ford Model T, talking to Eleanor. Seeing him standing there concerned me. Our whole deal had been based on the fact that he was out of the country. Had something changed? Was this some type of trick?

Anyway, Eleanor waved eagerly when she saw me. I waved back but wondered if I ought not just get back on the train. As I walked across the platform toward the car, several people watched with their eyes narrowed and their mouths agape, as if they had never seen a colored person before. The knot in my stomach tightened, but then my nerves relaxed. The man standing next to Eleanor was taller and several years younger than Mr. Fitzgerald. And then I saw a young colored woman, standing next to a truck with an older white couple. They didn't seem to notice me, but the young woman smiled and nodded when our eyes met. I felt relieved not to be the only colored woman in town. I should have asked her name.

The man standing with Eleanor was her attorney, Charles Gaston, though it wasn't clear why he was here. The three of us chatted easily as he drove us back to Eleanor's cottage. When we turned down the dirt road toward the house, I expected to see another white clapboard house like the others we had passed along the way. But Eleanor's cottage wasn't a cottage at all. It was a large two-story house made out of logs and fieldstone, surrounded on either side by trees. The lake peeked through the leaves like pieces of sky. A hint of fish and mud wafted through the air. It was hard to believe we were still in the state of New York.

I followed Eleanor into the house. Mr. Gaston grabbed my bags out of the car. Just inside of the door was a spacious kitchen with a two-burner, gas cook stove and small ice box. Then there was an open room with a huge picture window and a ceiling pitched to the roof like the inside of a church. The wood floors and walls made it feel as if you were still outside. Eleanor immediately started opening windows and pulling sheets off the furniture.

"Want me to stay and help you open up the house?" Mr. Gaston asked as he set my bags down near a little room just off the kitchen.

"Charles, it's sweet of you to offer, but there isn't much to do." Eleanor grabbed a sheet off the kitchen table. A billow of dust floated through the air.

"Are you sure Eleanor? It's an awful big house."

"Cora and I will manage just fine. Won't we Cora?" she asked with a forced cheerfulness.

"Yes, ma'am," I said, even though I had no idea what it meant to open up a house.

"I can stay," Mr. Gaston offered again.

"What about your *dinner*?" she asked.

"They won't miss me," he said.

Eleanor turned to me. "Cora, would you mind opening that door in the front room? It's quite warm in here."

"Of course," I said. They started to speak in hushed tones as soon as they thought I was out of earshot.

"Don't make this more difficult than it already is," she said.

"It doesn't have to be. I can stay. Help you get settled. I'll tell them my meeting ran late," he said.

I stepped out on the back porch to give them some more privacy. The view of the lake took my breath away. A few minutes later, I heard the back door bang against the frame so I went back in the house. Eleanor was upset about something. She stood over the kitchen sink, shoulders slumped, shaking her head. I pretended not to notice.

Opening the house up was a lot more work than Eleanor had indicated. In fact, she seemed genuinely surprised how much there was to do. There was dust everywhere. I found myself wishing Catherine was with us. She and I would have been able to open the house in half the time. Eleanor tried to help, but she just got in the way. After we cleaned the front room, Eleanor decided to call a woman she knew in town to clean the rest of the house. Two ladies arrived within the next hour. Eleanor and I moved upstairs to her bedroom.

Her things were packed in a large trunk. It looked as if she planned to stay at the cottage for the rest of her life. She started to unpack, but just seemed to be making a mess. I couldn't just watch, so I helped her put her things away.

"Cora, I didn't invite you here to be my servant. You're my guest. I can manage," she said.

I wondered how many other guests had ever helped to *open up* the house. "Many hands make light work," I said.

Truth be told, it was fun to go through her things. Her dresses felt like silk flower petals from a colorful garden. I could smell a hint of honeysuckle and spice as I hung them up in the closet. That may have come from one of the miniature bottles of perfume she had displayed on the bureau next to the window. When the sun hit them, they glistened like jewels.

I put the linens on her bed. When I turned to leave, Eleanor offered to help me set up my room. I told her I could manage. I expected to stay in the little room off the kitchen, but she insisted I take one of the guest rooms upstairs. I chose the corner room down the hall. It was the only room with a writing desk. Though it was quite a bit smaller than Eleanor's room, it still was larger than both the parlor and my bedroom back in Harlem.

After organizing Eleanor's closet, my few dresses looked so paltry. I don't know why I buy such drab colors. Maybe it's because I grew up listening to Mama complain about loose women and bright colors. If someone wore something too loud to church, she'd equate it to dressing like the devil. Respectable women wore clothes that didn't call any attention to themselves. Even the dress I bought to wear to the club was subdued, at least compared to most of the other women there that night, especially little-miss-too-orange. But it was more than just her dress. Everything about her said "look at me." I'm sure in the right situation that dress would have been very pretty, like the dresses in Eleanor's closet. I wonder if they have a sewing machine here. Maybe I'll make myself a new dress while I'm here.

Eleanor told me to make myself comfortable, even suggesting I might move the furniture around. I didn't think that would be necessary, but as I put things away, an overwhelming sense of freedom came over me. I suddenly wanted to do all I could to make the room feel like my own, even if it was only temporary. Oddly enough, rearranging the furniture reminded me of the freedom Edna felt moving out of her husband's house.

The writing desk is now by the window so I can see at the lake while I write. The moon's reflection on the surface is the most beautiful thing I have ever seen. I feel as if I could write forever. I can't wait to watch the sunrise in the morning.

June 19, 1928 (Chesterfield County)

I've been up here two full days and still haven't started working on my story. It's too quiet. Yesterday, while I was putting the groceries away, I actually heard the wind whistling through the trees. I never thought I would miss Junior and Dorothy fighting over the radio or Mr. Wright's heavy footsteps overhead. I even miss the sound of Earl's snoring. Honestly, I haven't been sleeping that well. I had that dream again last night. This time the man doesn't have a whip. He is standing over a woman, and I'm screaming for him to stop. Just as he comes charging for me, I wake up. I was so shaken; I couldn't get back to sleep. It doesn't help that the bed feels so big and empty.

It's strange to have so much time alone. I hardly know what to do. I find myself worried about things at home. Does Earl have enough supper before he leaves for work? Did he put his clothes out to be picked up by the laundry woman? How are the children faring in Georgia? Are they minding their manners? Do they have enough money? I wrote them each a letter. Hopefully, hearing back from them will ease my mind. It's not as easy as I thought it would be to put all of that aside.

Watching the mallards float along the top of the lake and listening to the wail of the loons is so relaxing. I could sit out here all day. I'm a little curious what it would be like to take one of the canoes out on the lake. But I'd be too afraid it would tip over. Besides, the oars are so heavy I don't think I would be able to maneuver them through the water. Eleanor goes canoeing every day. She says it's easier than it looks. I will just have to take her word for it.

June 20, 1928 (Chesterfield County)

I've spent the last hour trying to write about the sunrise, but my words pale in comparison to the view. Saying it's beautiful or that it shimmers lacks imagination. I'd love to paint a picture the way Langston did in "The Negro Speaks of Rivers." He describes the Mississippi so clearly, I can see it in my mind — "I heard the singing of the Mississippi when Abe Lincoln went down to New Orleans, and I've seen its muddy bosom turn all golden in the sunset."

I'm glad I brought *The Weary Blues* and a few other books up here with me. It gives me something to do when I'm not writing. I still haven't started working on my story. I can't seem to focus. I can't stop thinking about what happened the other day when Eleanor and I went into town for groceries.

I thought it odd that the Fitzgeralds don't have a car. They own one but only bring it up when Mr. Fitzgerald comes. Eleanor said she knows how to drive but doesn't have a license, which is why Mr. Gaston drove us from the train station on Saturday.

As we walked three miles up a steep incline in the blazing sun, I felt quite aggravated. I had to stop and catch my breath every few minutes. I tried to identify the wildflowers along the path to distract myself. I saw evening primrose, wild parsnip, verbena, sweet clover, and these purple flowers that look like daisies. A few yellow butterflies flew by. And every once in a while, glimmering cobalt blue water peeked out through the trees. Honestly, after a while the walk turned out to be rather pleasant despite the sun beating down on my gray dress. By the time we reached the edge of town, I was in much better spirits.

The town sits right on Seneca Lake, the largest of the Finger Lakes according to Eleanor. It smelled as if someone had scaled and gutted a thousand fish. Even the recently cut grass did little to mask it. There were six white clapboard houses — real cottages — three on each side of the street leading into town. Just as we reached the last house, the path changed from gravel to asphalt.

The center of town had a white gazebo with pink baskets of flowers hanging all around it. At the opposite end of town was a little white church just like the one they had back home in Georgia, except the paint wasn't chipping. The general store was the largest building in town, about twice the size of Daddy's store. It looked as if it could hold some of everything. The only thing it didn't have was a big porch on the front.

The tables inside the store were stacked high with apples, pears, blueberries, tomatoes, onions, beans and corn. Every shelf was completely stocked. Daddy could never keep his shelves full. Most people who shopped at his store paid on credit. I imagine the owner of this store never worried about people paying their bills. He looked pretty fancy in his long-sleeved blue shirt, red tie and gray vest. Even his crisp white apron looked more for show than part of his job. There were several young men stocking shelves and helping customers. The owner was in the back until he heard the clerk speak to Eleanor. He rushed out to greet her. When Eleanor introduced me, he nodded cordially to me, though his friendliness didn't quite make it to his eyes. I imagine things may have been a little different had I come in there alone.

Eleanor insisted on shopping for the food, so I wandered around the store picking up a few things for myself. I was looking through the bolts of fabric when I noticed that the clerk's stocking business seemed to coincide with whichever aisle I happened to be in. When I joined Eleanor, he only followed me with his eyes. She seemed completely unaware of the increased scrutiny and continued merrily filling her basket with enough food for a family of four. After she paid for the groceries, we walked across the town square to the soda shop for some ice cream.

"The Friendliest Ice Cream in the Whole State of New York" was written in red paint across the front window. I still can't figure out how ice cream can be friendly. The shop sat on the corner and had two big windows on either side of the door. There were two booths next to each window and several free-standing tables in the center. The five stools at the counter were the only ones that didn't have a view of the park.

The two young women sitting in the booth closest to the door barely looked up from their conversation when we walked in. I spoke as we passed by. I waited for a reaction to my presence, but nothing happened. No register of surprise. No disdain. No interest at all. They simply nodded and went back to their malts.

Eleanor and I sat at the counter. A woman came out of the kitchen with a pink flowered kerchief tied around her head and curly blonde hair sticking out the back. She looked to be about my age, but you never know with white women. They seem to age quicker. She was really excited to see Eleanor. She came around the counter to give her a hug.

"Miss Eleanor, it's so good to see you! Where are the boys?" she asked.

"They are in France with Arthur's mother. I'm here alone — well, except for my friend, Cora."

The woman's face reddened at the word friend. I thought to myself, *now we're getting back on familiar ground*. But then she smiled and extended

119

her hand to me. "Any friend of Miss Eleanor's is a friend of mine," she said, introducing herself as Margaret.

After a bit of catching up, Margaret went back behind the counter. She gave each of us a bowl of her "friendly ice cream." The only difference between her friendly ice cream and the frozen custard Mama used to make was it didn't melt as fast.

"Margaret, your ice cream is still the best in the land."

"Thank you, Miss Eleanor. My father's recipe. I haven't changed a thing."

"Old family recipes are the best. I think they appreciated the food more back in those days," Eleanor paused, with her spoon hovering above her bowl as if suddenly remembering something. "Cora, one of your peach pies would be perfect with Margaret's ice cream. You must make one while we are up here."

"Of course," I said.

Eleanor took another spoonful of ice cream. "Let's make two so Margaret can have one."

"Sure," I said, wondering when we were going to have time to make pies once I started writing.

"Make a few and I'll sell them. People love homemade pie," Margaret added.

"Oh, she won't have time to make more than one or two. Cora is up here to work on a project."

"Well, I'm sure that will keep her plenty busy while she's here," Margaret replied as if I weren't there.

The conversation changed to local gossip. I wondered what type of project Margaret thought I was working on. Not that it was any of her business. I just didn't want her thinking I had come all this way to clean their cottage.

Margaret scooped herself a bowl of ice cream and sat down with us. Not once have I seen Millie in Harlem come from behind the counter to sit with a customer. She's always busy either cooking or serving food. And when she's not doing that, she's cleaning. Not to mention she isn't the friendliest woman. But then people might think that about me when I'm at the library. You don't have time to be friendly when you know people are watching and waiting for you to make a mistake. I can't even imagine what Millie has to do to keep her place open.

As I ate my ice cream, I felt a sense of leisure I'd never felt before. There wasn't anything I needed to do. No one needed me. I just sat there enjoying my ice cream without a care in the world. But then Eleanor asked about Margaret's husband.

The smile on Margaret's face dissolved. "He's out of town," she said.

"Oh. I'm sorry to have missed him. How long will he be gone?"

"I'm not sure," Margaret said, dumping Eleanor's leftover ice cream into her bowl and then stacking it on top of hers.

"That's frustrating. Not knowing when Arthur will return leaves me on edge."

There was a sudden chill in the air. I tried to change the subject by reminding Eleanor we needed to pick up the groceries before it got too late, but she ignored me.

"Well, I hope to see him before I leave," Eleanor said, not seeming to notice the strain on Margaret's face.

Margaret stood up. "He's not coming back."

"What?"

"He's gone. He isn't coming back."

"Oh, my word. What on earth happened?"

"It's just one of those things," Margaret replied vaguely. She walked back behind the counter, temples pulsating. There was clearly more to the story than she wanted to share.

Eleanor followed her behind the counter. "Is there anything I can do to help you?" she asked, putting her arm around Margaret.

Margaret sighed heavily. "No. There isn't."

"Marriage can be difficult, but Ben is a good man. I'm sure things will work themselves out," Eleanor said, squeezing Margaret's shoulder

"It won't," Margaret replied flatly. She shook her head, sighing again. "Ben was always a gambler. Nothing too big. The drawer would come up short sometimes, but he always put it back. But then six months ago things got so bad we lost our house. We moved into the apartment upstairs. A few weeks later, he took the little money we had in savings and left town."

"Oh, Margaret! I'm so sorry," Eleanor said, hugging her tighter.

"I wish that was the worst of it. He mortgaged the shop and now I have a week to come up with the back payments or I'll lose it," she said as she wiped the tears on her cheek with the corner of her apron. They stood there wordlessly for a while as Margaret cried. She finally pulled away from Eleanor's embrace and grabbed a napkin to blow her nose.

"My father built this shop and worked his entire life to make sure we owned it free and clear," Margaret said.

"Your father was such an industrious man," Eleanor added.

"It breaks my heart to think of someone else running it."

Margaret explained her plan to close after the weekend and move in with her sister in Cleveland. Eleanor nodded as she listened, but her pressed lips and furrowed eyebrows suggested her mind was somewhere else. She looked around the shop and after a few minutes nodded again. Then she squared her shoulders.

"May I take a look in the kitchen?" she asked.

"Sure, Miss Eleanor."

The two women disappeared behind the light blue curtain that separated the shop from the kitchen. I sat there trying to digest everything Margaret had shared when she came out of the kitchen without Eleanor. She didn't say anything or even look my way. It must have been awkward for her to share her private business with a stranger. I wanted to say something that would make her feel better. But what could I say? The only thing I could do was give her some privacy.

I stood up and went to the window. There were more people on the square than earlier. Two women chatted while their children ran after a ball. I hoped they wouldn't decide to come in for ice cream while Margaret was still so visibly upset.

Eleanor finally came out of the kitchen. "Margaret, I have a solution. I will pay the back payments and the rest of the mortgage. That way you can keep your shop. We will be partners."

Eleanor's words hung in the air like a dense fog. Margaret didn't move or say anything. She just stood there with her hand over her mouth. I felt as surprised as Margaret looked. One minute Eleanor is eating ice cream, the next she is buying the entire soda shop.

Margaret finally spoke. "Miss Eleanor, that's a generous offer, but it's my problem. I'll figure something out."

"For once in my life I want to act on instinct instead of propriety. Let me do this." She paused and looked at me for the first time since coming out of the kitchen. "You will be saving me from drowning."

It was as if she was Edna Pontellier, standing naked in the open air before the ocean. But I feared Eleanor's generosity was as dangerous as walking out into the sea. I wondered if Mr. Fitzgerald shared her enthusiasm for helping poor women, white or black.

Margaret and Eleanor went back and forth about the offer, but eventually Margaret agreed. As they were discussing the details, the women from the park came in for ice cream and sat as far as they possibly could away from where I stood. As Eleanor and I were leaving, I had the urge to tell them I made the ice cream.

We stopped at the post office for Eleanor to telegram Mr. Gaston. As she dictated the message, there was a strange fluttering in my stomach. Something didn't feel right. I wanted to suggest she talk to Mr. Fitzgerald first. But I was pretty sure we didn't have that kind of relationship. As we walked back to the house, Eleanor's looming purchase weighed me down a lot more than the bags of groceries. Why is Eleanor giving away so much money? It can't be good.

June 23, 1928
Chesterfield County, New York

Dear Langston,

Today marks one week at the cottage. My days are divided between reading and writing. I have finished a few books, though nothing worth mentioning. One ending was too ambiguous. Another one ended with the death of a character, which I always find quite distressing.

Eleanor and I are getting along quite well, though I am concerned about her decision to buy the soda shop in town. The owner's husband mortgaged it to cover his gambling debts, but didn't keep up with the payments. Then he left town. I know Eleanor means well, but I once overheard Mr. Fitzgerald reprimand her about giving money to some women's club. Do you think it's odd that she has such an interest in sponsoring other women?

My writing is going very well, though I don't have anything complete enough to send to you. How is your novel coming?

Warmest Regards,

Cora

June 24, 1928 (Chesterfield County)

I received a letter from Earl today. It made me happy to see my name written in his handwriting. He said he missed me and that he made a mistake allowing me to go. It annoyed me. And yet as much as I want to assert that I am a grown woman capable of making my own decisions, I would not have come had he not *allowed* it. Why do men have so much control over women?

Nevertheless, it eased my mind to know that Mrs. Johnson leaves him a meal every day. He suspects she has been snooping when she drops the food off. I'm sure of it. She always knows a little too much about other people's business. But she's a good Christian woman who is always willing to help. Her nosiness is a small price to pay. Fortunately, Earl put our private papers away in our bedroom.

Overall, he's seems to be faring well. He is even considering auditioning at the Cotton Club. I doubt he will do it, though. He gets a cut from the nightly tally at Rueben's and wouldn't make as much money. But imagine if he got to play with Duke Ellington's orchestra. That would be incredible.

There was one other thing that troubled me. He mentioned taking some of our savings and the money Eleanor is paying me to buy a part of the club as an investment. And even though he told me not to fret because it was just an idea, he never asked me what I thought and definitely did not ask for my approval. It reminded me of how Margaret's husband made the decision to mortgage the soda shop.

I know scripture says, "Wives, submit to your own husbands, as to the Lord. For the husband is head of the wife, as also Christ is head of the church. . . ", but it gets tiresome always having someone over you. I guess I should be happy most of the letter was about how much he loved me and missed me.

June 27, 1928 (Chesterfield County)

There's a wine cellar underneath the cottage with cases and cases of wine. After dinner, we grabbed a bottle and sat by the lake to watch the sunset. I don't know if it was the alcohol or not, but I asked Eleanor why she bought Margaret's shop.

"Why not? I have the money," she said.

"I know, but won't Mr. Fitzgerald be upset?" I asked.

Eleanor reached for the bottle between us and refilled her glass. She sipped on her wine, staring at the lake. The question hung above us like the sword of Damocles.

"Of course he will. But there won't be anything he can do about it. All the papers will be signed well before he returns from Europe."

Nothing in her tone suggested that she was the least bit worried about stirring up her husband's anger. He seemed quite particular about how she spent his money. If he didn't want her donating to a women's club, he certainly wouldn't want her buying a whole business. It's like what Aunt Lucy said about Agnes: "The wise woman builds her house, but the foolish pulls it down with her hands."

Though to be honest, I am in no position to judge. Being here might tear down my house if Earl knew I was lounging by the lake, drinking wine. It wouldn't matter one bit what I wanted to accomplish. All he would care about is that I sent our children off to my brother's and left him in the care of a neighbor. But what choice did I have? I was drowning.

"To making our own decisions," I said, raising my glass in the air.

"To taking risks," she said, touching her glass to mine.

We finished the first bottle and Eleanor went back down to the cellar to get another one. When she came back, she sat on the edge of the ottoman in front of my chair. "You want to know why I'm buying Margaret's shop?" she asked.

"Yes," I said.

"Have you ever heard of the Heterodoxy?"

I shook my head.

"It's a ladies' luncheon club that meets every other Saturday down in Greenwich Village. It isn't like any other group I have ever been involved with. The women are all so different. The only thing we have in common is our unorthodox way of thinking. There are women in the club who are very open about their involvement with other women. And women who. . ."

"Involvement?"

"You know, sexually."

My mind flashed back to Mr. Fitzgerald yelling at her about consorting with the likes of some jezebels. I thought he meant women who were not up to his social standing given that people with money often think they are better than people without. But that wasn't it at all. I wondered if Eleanor invited me to her cottage for more than just my writing.

"I know what you're thinking," Eleanor said as if she were reading my mind. "While it isn't what I would choose for myself, it isn't at all what people assume it is. They aren't sick or perverted. They fall in love and care for one another the same way you or I might fall in love and care for a man."

It didn't sound the same to me at all, though I nodded my head in agreement as she continued to talk.

"Listening to those women tell their stories helped me to understand that love is love. The same thing happened when I heard the woman from Harlem tell her story. She taught me that Negro women and white women have many of the same struggles."

I sipped my wine, doubting the woman from Harlem that she met was your ordinary colored woman. It was probably someone like Mrs. W.E.B. Du Bois. The typical colored woman didn't have time or money for a luncheon every other week.

"It's liberating to be able to discuss politics, or women's rights or literature or even sexuality without castigation. Everything we talk about stays at the meeting. We can't even take notes. So it's safe to share your personal thoughts, which is a good thing since we're all required to give these talks about our life called background talks. You wouldn't believe the tragedies and horrors women have had to endure."

"I can imagine," I said, thinking about the stories I've heard during prayer meetings and from the women in my building.

"It breaks my heart. And yet, I'm always inspired by their strength and courage."

"My mother used to say, *God comforts us so we can turn around and comfort others*," I said.

"I never thought of it that way. It's almost as if the trials and tribulations have a purpose."

"It's too bad that's the only way we learn to help one another," I said, wondering what this had to do with her buying Margaret's shop.

"True. But even the talks about adventure and travel inspired me to want to do more and see more. All of them made me nervous to present my talk. I couldn't imagine anyone being inspired or even interested in my dull life."

I thought about the woman on the train. She probably was embarrassed by the way her husband spoke to her in front of the other people, but her tears inspired so much of the main character in the story I've been working on.

"We don't always know when we are inspiring someone," I said.

Eleanor turned away as she drained the wine in her glass. "That may well be true, but we definitely know when we are boring someone."

"I'm sure it was better than you thought."

She shook her head. "It wasn't, but the ladies were gracious. They listened attentively. There were even a few who came up to the podium at the end to congratulate me, but it was too late. The glassy-eyed stares of the audience were already etched on my brain. As I walked out of the meeting that day, I resolved to do more with my life than just be someone's wife and mother."

I still didn't quite understand how it all related to the money she was giving away. But her mood had changed, so it didn't feel right to ask. "I would love to hear your talk."

Eleanor stood up and shook her head. "I couldn't bear to go through it again." She set her glass down and went in the house.

I knew she needed a friend to encourage her, but the wine and the sunset made it difficult to move. I sat back in my chair and watched the last band of orange sunlight slip beneath the surface of the lake, leaving behind a sky of indigo. I would have stayed out there all night if it weren't for all the critters and whatnot.

June 28, 1928 (Chesterfield County)

When I came downstairs this morning to make breakfast, Eleanor's background talk was on the table with a note — *You trusted me.* Reading it felt a bit like prying into someone's most private life.

She started by describing her parents' marriage, which sounded about like my parents in that they didn't have any real affection or love for one another. Her mother had the place in New York high society and her father had the money. The only other comment she made about growing up was that her father really wanted sons.

Then she wrote about traveling and studying art in France as a young woman but wasn't very descriptive about where she traveled. I wanted to be able to imagine myself in those places. She also didn't mention anything about the painting techniques she learned or an explanation of what she painted or why. Of course, that would have made the talk more interesting but not more inspiring. Inspiration comes from courage in the face of danger or loss.

Eleanor's description of Mr. Fitzgerald and their marriage was puzzling. She never mentioned anything about love, only that she had to do what was expected. She wrote about how their personalities complemented one another and how his blue eyes reminded her of the sea on a clear day. But then she described him as haughty and autocratic, adding that he had forbidden her to give any more money to the organization. However, it turns out it's her money. Mr. Fitzgerald is the executor of her trust. He administers her monthly allowance because her father didn't believe women capable of managing money.

I stopped reading it for a while because it irritated me how much easier life was for white people, especially rich white people. Her monthly allowance is probably ten times more than Earl and I make combined. And yet she's unhappy because Mr. Fitzgerald controls it. But then it occurred to me that maybe it had more to do with a man lording over her. No different than Earl giving me permission to come up here.

No surprise Eleanor saw herself in Edna. They are much more alike than Edna and me. Though we both identify with Edna's feelings about moving through the motions of life, Eleanor also sought a young man to awaken her passion. I wonder if that was Mr. Gaston. Or was there someone else? Why a woman would want the headache of two men is beyond me. Maybe it's the newness of the relationship. When you're married with children it's hard to give each other time. I must admit there have been times when I've wondered what it would be like to be wooed by a man other than Earl, but then I remember what the Bible says — looking at someone with lust is committing adultery in your heart.

The talk ended with a vow to make a difference in the world and become the woman she was meant to be. I wasn't quite sure what that meant, but I didn't have the opportunity to ask Eleanor about it. She didn't come down for breakfast. And when I got back from my walk, she had gone out. I might have spent more time thinking about her talk if I hadn't gotten a letter from Dorothy.

It made me smile when I read about how much she was enjoying cooking, and how the children weren't as bad as she thought they would be. She even wrote about wearing a big floppy hat and looking like a real country girl. She said Junior is a lot happier than he admits. He works all day with Harold and then goes with him to the general store to drink whiskey. I didn't love the idea of Junior drinking but at least it's with his uncle and not those hoodlums in Harlem. Dorothy also wrote about hating the outhouse and how her brother told her there were snakes in there. She tried to get Junior to write to me, but he told her to say hello for him. She was very happy that she received a letter from her father. It is such a relief to know they have settled in and are enjoying themselves.

Lincoln University
Pennsylvania
June 30, 1928

Dear Cora,

Wealthy New York socialites love having a pet project. It makes them feel as if they are giving back to the community. Most of the time it's in the form of this or that society, but I have heard of some who like to take on an individual as their cause.

What you overheard between Eleanor and her husband was probably related to the politics of the women's movement and not money. I'm sure her investment in the soda shop is barely enough for Mr. Fitzgerald to notice. Or maybe she has her own money. Either way I wouldn't worry too much about it.

I'm glad you have had time to read. I recently finished Miss Fauset's new novel <u>Plum Bun</u>. *I didn't care for the theme. It disturbs me to read about Negroes passing for white. I have always felt their encounters weren't genuine. Rather than interacting from the authentic position of their own experience, they assume the persona of a white person. They don't further the communication between the races. They just pretend there's only one way to approach life and anyone who doesn't fit the mold doesn't deserve to attend the party.*

It isn't like your experience at the cottage. You have the opportunity to observe white American life from the inside without sacrificing who you are. I'd imagine spending time up there as Eleanor's friend is extremely interesting and a lot of fun.

My writing is going well. I spent the last few weeks developing short histories for all my characters — where they were born, things that happened to them or what might happen to them. I am just now beginning to work on the story itself. I had hoped to get the entire thing done before school starts again, but there just isn't enough time in the day.

How is your writing coming along? I am anxious to see what you are working on. Write as soon as you can.

Respectfully,

Langston

July 1, 1928 (Chesterfield County)

I can't stop thinking about Eleanor's background. How does giving Margaret and me money make a difference in the world? I've tried to ask her about it, but she changes the subject whenever I bring up the background talk. I tried to give it back to her, but she told me to keep it.

I haven't made much progress with Rose and the cardinal story. I write paragraphs and paragraphs, but they don't go anywhere. The wastepaper basket next to my desk is full of crumpled up paper. Maybe I should try Langston's idea of short histories that he mentioned in his last letter. I need to know more about Rose's history to write her story.

What if Charlotte from "A Cup of Coffee" became Rose? I know a bit more about her. She likes books and works in the library. But it doesn't make sense for Rose to work. It will just get in the way. She can still have a friendship Everett, but she's not married to him. She's married to a prominent banker, but maybe that's too much like Mr. Fitzgerald. He could be a musician, but they don't make enough money. Rose is married to someone who has a lot of money. A doctor maybe. And they have a son and a daughter two years apart.

Something has changed or happened in their marriage to make her unhappy. Eleanor's talk mentioned Mr. Fitzgerald was more interested in his work than their marriage. Maybe he is absent a lot or preoccupied. Earl gets that way when business is bad at the club or he is working on his music. He's moody and easily irritated. Even though I know it doesn't have anything to do with me it still makes me feel bad. It usually doesn't last too long. What if that's part of Rose's husband's personality though? Eleanor described Mr. Fitzgerald as haughty and autocratic in her talk. That would be a challenge to live with. But maybe what troubles her is more than her marriage. Perhaps she is dissatisfied with her life and her choices.

Rose tries to make herself feel better, but nothing works. She bought new clothes, cut her hair into a bob, and even took art classes, but none of it helped. What if one afternoon she decides she needs a holiday? A trip to the beach.

Sounds too much like *The Awakening*. Maybe I should go back to Pearl and Sylvia as characters. They are more familiar. I understand who they are and have an easier time writing about them.

July 2, 1928 (Chesterfield County)

I tried writing about Pearl and Sylvia, but it reminds me too much of every other story or book I've read about colored people. It's always the same. Growing up poor in the South. The family doing all they can to survive. Being belittled and mistreated by white folks. Living in constant fear that some violence will be perpetrated against you or someone you love for no other reason than the color of your skin. It breaks my heart. We have been through so much as a people, but we have endured. I guess that's why I think racism and oppression shouldn't be our only focus. There are other stories to tell.

Too bad the pages in this journal can't to be submitted for the contest. I've definitely written a lot in here. I need to get back to work on my story. But where do I even start? I keep coming back to Eleanor's background talk hoping it will help. But even after reading it over and over again I don't feel I know her any better. Something is missing.

If I wrote a background talk, I would talk about the things you don't tell everybody. After all, she said it was a place to be open. I would share how Earl and I came from families where our fathers always had other women. Earl's father eventually left his mother with a bunch of children. We made a promise we would never let that be an issue in our marriage. Sometimes I worry about him working late at the club around all those women, but I think about who he is as a man. The day we first meet we were both reading *The Souls of Black Folk* in Central Park. I felt a spark of excitement as we discussed our personal experience with the double consciousness of always seeing ourselves through the eyes of whites that Dr. Du Bois described in his book. Our courtship was filled with deep conversations, music and long nights in one another's arms. We were definitely in love. Together we were going to live beyond the conventions of typical Negro life. He was going to make his way as a musician. I was going to be a writer. But reality settled in after Junior was born. One of us had to have a dependable job. The library hardly felt like a concession on my part. I loved spending my days surrounded by books. I barely noticed my dream fading into the distance.

Maybe that's too personal.

July 3, 1928 (Chesterfield County)

Eleanor has spent the last few days with Mr. Gaston. She leaves right after breakfast and doesn't come back until well after dinner. She says they are working on the particulars of buying Margaret's shop, which I know isn't the whole story. But I decided it wasn't any of my business.

The nice thing about Eleanor's absence is I can read for hours without a single soul bothering me. But to be honest, I miss my family. I plan to call them tomorrow for the Fourth of July.

Yesterday when Eleanor asked how my writing was going, I felt guilty. I haven't written anything in two days. She suggested I might need some time to sit back and just think. I've decided to take a break from writing until after the holiday.

July 17, 1928 (Chesterfield County)

Well, it's done. Eleanor owns Margaret's soda shop. Mr. Gaston brought the papers out to the cottage last night for her to sign. Eleanor invited him to stay for supper and insisted on cooking herself. She picked a recipe from her cookery book and managed to get all the ingredients assembled on the counter. But once she turned the stove on, the only thing she made was a horrible mess. I tried to help, but she refused.

Mr. Gaston sat in the living room reading a magazine, seemingly unaffected by the haze of smoke filling the house. When she finally served the food, the beef tasted a bit like tree bark and the vegetables were almost raw. Mr. Gaston ate every bite, which is more than I can say for me or Eleanor. Neither of us ate more than a mouthful. Fortunately, we had some chocolate cake left over from a few days ago for dessert.

Mr. Gaston smoked a cigar while Eleanor and I put the food away and cleaned the kitchen. Then we all played cribbage and drank wine until sunset. The two of them were still sitting out by the lake when I went to bed around ten.

When I came down in the morning, Eleanor was already up. "I should have let you make supper last night. I don't know what got into me," she said as she poured me a cup of coffee.

"Supper wasn't that bad."

"Oh, Cora! If it wasn't for that chocolate cake, you and I would have had no supper at all."

"Well, Mr. Gaston seemed to enjoy himself."

"He did. But I think we should have him back tonight for a proper supper."

"Sure," I said, wondering why she felt the need to keep up pretenses.

I spent the rest of the day writing, though the story is a long way from being finished. It's so hard to get the ideas in my head to make sense on paper. And there are still parts of it I haven't been able to figure out. It seems strange that I don't know what's going to happen next in the story. Maybe it's because I'm new at this. I'm sure real writers like Langston know exactly where their stories are going.

Chesterfield County, New York
July 21, 1928

Dear Langston,

I had no idea writing was such hard work. There are days when I can't find the right words to express the thoughts in my head. I type and type but nothing makes sense. Then there are the days when everything flows. Hours will pass without me even realizing it. But then I go back to what I've written, and it doesn't seem quite right. The back and forth is like nothing I have ever done before. It is exhilarating and frustrating all at the same time.

Eleanor has been a great help. The days when I'm most frustrated she encourages me to take a walk or invites me to go with her to visit Margaret. Those little outings always help to get me back on track.

I borrowed your idea of creating a short history for my character. It took me quite a few days to figure out all the details. Like you said in your last letter, there isn't enough time in the day.

My story is finally finished. I have enclosed a copy of "The Cardinal" for you to read. I'm anxious to hear what you think. Please include any suggestions you have. I hope to send it off to <u>Opportunity</u> well before the August 31st deadline.

Things are so easygoing up here; I hate to think about going home. I've received a few letters from my family. They are enjoying their summer, but everyone is anxious to get back to normal. I'm not sure things will ever be normal for me again. Waking up to the loons and going through my day without any expectations is the way life ought to be. I can't imagine listening to the street noise in Harlem or rushing down Lenox to work. It's all too confining. I suppose I should just enjoy the last few weeks up here. "No thought for the morrow. Sufficient unto the day."

Hope you are getting a chance to enjoy the lazy days of summer.

Best regards,

Cora

The Cardinal

By Cora James

A cardinal sat perched on a low-hanging branch outside the kitchen window. Its bright red tail feathers flung over the side of the bough like the train of an evening gown.

"What-cheer, what-cheer. Tchip, tchip"

Rose glanced up at the tree through the folds of the draperies. The bird seemed to be looking straight at her. Its red feathers shouted through the green of the leaves, pay attention — I'm important.

It felt odd to be drawn to a bird. Their fluttering wings reminded her of the panic she felt whenever her grandmother's canary flew out of its ornate brass cage. When she asked for the door to be closed, her grandmother would stretch out her finger to call for the bird. It has the right to freedom, she'd say. But flying around the parlor didn't give the bird freedom, especially since it always wound up back in its cage.

The thought troubled Rose. Like the canary, she could only do so much or go so far. Her life was controlled by the expectations and restrictions of being a woman. She learned early to comply and not question, silencing the desires of her heart. But like the cardinal, she longed to be free. She wanted more for herself.

Change seemed to be the only thing on her mind the past three months since she joined the Heterodoxy. Though the women came from various walks of life, their radical thinking drew them together. The conversations challenged Rose's thinking and roused her soul. She longed to forge her own path — a path that mattered. A path built on more than the beliefs and traditions of the past. A path far away from the life she'd always known.

When these thoughts first surfaced, Rose worried that she might be losing her mind. After all, who wouldn't want her life? A wealthy husband. A beautiful home. A closet full of the latest fashions. Lavish trips. But none of those things were a result of her own efforts. All the important decisions were made for her. She didn't even have a say over her own children. That was the nanny's domain. She had to free herself.

Rose returned to her seat at the kitchen table and picked up the notes she had written and read aloud:

> Like many of you, I recently read Kate Chopin's The Awakening. I see myself in Edna. I see the ways in which I move through the motions of my life. And it seemed, like Edna, I needed a young man to awaken my passion. However, I realize what I want is Edna's courage to risk comfort for fulfillment.

Rose paused, laying her notes back on the table and thought of Everett. That day in the park it seemed as if destiny had brought them together when she realized he was also reading Leaves of Grass. Had she really felt a charge when their hands touched?

The first few months of their affair had been thriving. Even the mundane cocktail parties and dinners she attended with Robert were more bearable after an afternoon spent staring into Everett's hazel eyes. The sparkle of his eyes, like the golden sun along the crisp aqua sea, aroused a deep passion that burned long after they parted ways. She could barely contain herself between their trysts.

But the excitement waned as they spent more time together. He criticized her lunch selections.

Instead of long conversations about an imagined future together, he talked excessively about himself and his business. Rose would listen patiently, but tired of feigning interest. She didn't understand why her husband and lover were more alike than different.

It hadn't been easy to end their relationship. Everett wanted an opportunity to prove his love. When she insisted they stop seeing one another, he threatened to expose their relationship. For months, she had lived in fear, but stood her ground. Her role as wife and mother consumed her. She no longer had a place where she belonged to herself.

Rose picked up the notes off the table, folded them in half and stuck them in her pocket.

* * *

Rose fumbled nervously with the sheets of paper in front of her as she watched women mill around Polly's Café. What if they found her talk boring? There was nothing particularly exciting about her life. And the only risk she'd ever taken wasn't even included in her talk. It would be too humiliating to share her sexual indiscretion. She hoped she wouldn't sound as pathetic as she felt.

Elizabeth, the chairwoman of the club, stepped to the podium and tapped the gavel three times. The voices tapered off until there was quiet in the room.

"Good afternoon, ladies. First, I'd like to welcome our new members and guests. We are very pleased you have chosen to spend the afternoon with us. Please remember anything discussed must not leave this room. We want everyone to have the freedom to speak openly without fear of repercussions from their spouses or the public.

"Today we have several women who will share their background talks. For those new to the Heterodoxy, these talks are designed to share our experiences of growing up as a female in this world. They also allow us to understand how our backgrounds determine the women we become. Our first speaker is Rose Avery. Rose has been a member for six months. We are so excited to have the opportunity to hear her story. Please join me in welcoming Rose to the podium."

The room exploded into applause. Rose's heart raced as she tried to stand, her knees suddenly losing their strength. She took a deep breath and mounted the steps of the stage. Though her shoulders were relaxed and her dress swayed as if a gentle breeze passed through the room, her silver sandals felt as if they contained lead. Elizabeth nodded slightly as their eyes met. Rose settled her papers on the podium and looked out at the audience.

Her hands shook as she cleared her throat. "This looks much easier from the audience."

The women chuckled.

Rose sighed, and then started with her earliest memories of growing up in New York. She noticed a woman nodding off in the back of the room as she talked about her family's business. It was only when she shifted to her love of books and dream of being a writer that the audience seemed to come alive. Rose even noticed a few women nodding and smiling.

"It's difficult to completely articulate the sense of satisfaction I felt whenever I finished a story. But books weren't valued by my family. So, I stopped writing. Soon my only connection to books was frequent visits to the library for booklover's club." Rose paused and looked down at her notes. No one cares about the cotillions she attended or her mother's attempt to parade her in front of every eligible bachelor. They wanted authenticity. She folded her notes in half and took a deep breath.

"I hadn't planned to talk much about my marriage, but it seems disingenuous to keep it a secret when many of you have shared so deeply. I met my husband on a visit to an art gallery. We were both drawn to the same painters. And oddly enough our interest in art and museums made for some wonderful afternoons, which eventually led to marriage. But the realities of life changed us both. He soon only focused on his work. And I did what was expected of me as a wife and a mother."

Rose went on to explain how her father made her husband the executor of her trust. "My inheritance is what enabled him to start his own practice. The rest he doles out in monthly increments. I spent most of that money at boutiques and millinery shops, but then a year ago I decided to start saving it. And as my account grew, I felt a sense of satisfaction. But lately I want more than a nest egg in the bank."

* * *

Though several women thanked Rose for sharing her story, no one called it inspirational or moving. She managed to get through the rest of the luncheon without tears, but she couldn't hide her disappointment when Elizabeth asked if the talk had gone as she had planned.

"I'm afraid my story wasn't very interesting."

"We don't always know when we are inspiring someone, Rose. Not many women in your position would be willing to risk their comfort for fulfillment. Someone here today needed to hear your message."

142

"Thank you, Elizabeth. That's very kind."

"Rose, I never waste time on platitudes. Most stories shared in these meetings are told after the fact. Your story is only the beginning. You have more power than you realize. That money is a seed waiting to take root." Another member tapped Elizabeth on the shoulder and whispered in her ear. Elizabeth nodded and then excused herself.

Rose wanted nothing more than to leave the café, but a group of women stood in front of the door talking. She couldn't bear to hear any more comments about her talk, so she sat down at an empty table. Tears moistened her lashes.

Polly, the owner of the restaurant, started clearing off a nearby table, dumping the dirty dishes and glasses into a small tub. "I loved hearing about your love of books and writing. What were your stories about?" she asked, seeming not to notice Rose's tears.

Rose quickly dabbed the corners of her eyes. "People I knew growing up."

"I've wanted to write poetry." Polly paused and looked away.

Rose didn't respond in hopes that it be the end of their conversation.

Polly sat the tub on the table and continued. "As a girl I would sit under the oak tree behind our house and read for hours. I especially loved Emily Dickinson."

Rose offered a weak smile.

"Don't have much time for that type of thing nowadays," Polly said sadly as she started to pick up dishes again.

Rose wanted to say something encouraging, but nothing came to mind. All she could think of was the numerous ways she'd tried to change her own life and failed. The only joy she felt was tossing seeds to the birds at the park. She loved watching the birds fly up into the trees with the collected pieces in their mouths. It made her feel as if she'd made a difference.

The gruff sound of a man's voice startled Rose, interrupting her thoughts. A man in a gray three-piece suit stood over Polly as she looked through some papers. His expression looked as if he were lecturing a child. Polly picked up the papers and nodded.

"I understand," she said.

"One week," he said, before turning to leave the restaurant.

Polly nodded. She stood stoic until the door closed behind him, and then her shoulders slumped.

"What's wrong?" Rose asked.

Polly looked up, surprised. "Nothing. Everything is fine," she said, wiping her eyes with the corner of her apron.

Rose noticed the word "foreclosure" written in red on the top of the papers in Polly's hand. "Are you sure?" she asked as she stood up.

Polly stuffed the papers in her hand into her apron pocket. "Yes, I'm sure. Just some business I need to take care of."

Rose nodded. "I hope you don't mind if I stay for a bit."

"No. Stay as long as you like," Polly said as she began collecting plates again.

Rose watched Polly walk back and forth into the kitchen with piles of dirty dishes. It never occurred to her two women from such different stations in life could feel that same exact way. But she recognized the look of bewilderment on Polly's face. It was how she felt when Robert chastised her for spending too much money. She had often cried powerless tears. It would be such a loss for the women of the Heterodoxy if Polly's Café closed.

Rose picked up the cups and saucers still left on the tables. 'If only I could help,' she thought as she carried the dishes through the little blue curtain into the kitchen. Standing in the doorway she couldn't help but notice how different the kitchen was from her own. There were no windows and it smelled of built-up grease and dirt. Her shoes stuck slightly to the ground as she walked across the floor. It was a wonder the food that came out of here was edible.

Polly stood hunched over the sink running hot water over the dishes. Rose set the items she had collected on the counter then went over to the opened screen door. There wasn't much to look at other than the building across the alley. No oak trees with cardinals to offer hope.

"Thank you for helping," Polly said, untying her apron and hanging it on the hook next to the door.

"I wish I could do more."

Rose turned to leave, shoving her hands in the pockets of her coat. The tips of her fingers grazed the leftover seeds from her trip to the park.

Could it be that simple? Rose wondered as she glanced around the kitchen.

A painting of a cardinal on the wall caught her attention. Her heart fluttered. Her seeds would take root and make a difference.

Lincoln University
Pennsylvania
July 28, 1928

Dear Cora,

I just finished reading "The Cardinal" and felt compelled to write at once. I'll start by saying the writing was superb. It shows the work of a real writer. For that I commend you.

However, I have a real concern about your chosen theme and treatment. I know a writer must write from their heart, expressing the truth as he or she sees it. Yet, I can't help but believe as Negro writers we have a larger responsibility to our community. We are the voice for a people who have been silenced for centuries. We must honestly represent the struggle of our people, not minimize it.

You found The Sport of the Gods *difficult to read because you were able to connect to Dunbar's truth. You suggested a female writer would have shown more hope in the story. I found your comments intriguing and thought you would write a story where I would see the black woman's strength and perseverance. I wanted insight into how she processes this country's inclination to exclude us from the American table.*

From a literary perspective, it's our responsibility to use our art as a way to reflect on life as Negro in America and to represent those who came before us. We can't let privilege or education separate us from the average colored person. We are all black.

Our people may be uneducated and poor, but there is much we can learn from what they have seen and all they have survived. Those old black women on the first bench in church. Their slender fingers with the folds of wrinkled skin look frail, but when they take hold of your hand you can feel the strength of generations. These stories get lost when we buy into the standardization of America. White isn't all there is. It doesn't give credit to the very people on whose backs this country was built. And if we as writers give into this even subconsciously, we lose credibility. We further exclude the average colored person from the story of this country.

A Negro writer can't make it seem as if it were no big deal to be black or to have black experiences. We must fight the urge to be more and more white. As if being white is right and being a Negro is inherently wrong. I understand this may not have been your intention. But I fear your story might give whites the impression they are correct in believing the "Negro problem" would be easily corrected if Negroes would just learn to be more like them. It waters down the beauty of the Negro people, and more importantly it thwarts any chance of understanding.

It's like when I watch Earl stand on stage. His music becomes the expression of Negro life. He doesn't try to imagine the music from the perspective of a white man that has it all. No. When he plucks out the beat on his bass, he digs deep in his soul from his personal experience as a black man. And the beat . . . oh the beat, like tribal tom-toms, reach back across the ocean all the way to our ancestral Africa. You feel centuries of spirituality. The joy and laughter, as well as the pain, reflected in every face. If you deny that in your writing you are running away from the quintessence of your own people.

There is no virtue in being white, though I know it can be tempting to think there is. Experiencing the finer things can be very intoxicating. You might be inclined to believe life would be better if you were more like them or if you have the luxuries they have. Who can argue with the ease of going into a restaurant and being treated like a human being? I loved that about living in Mexico. No one cared about the color of my skin. I was free to be whoever and do whatever I wanted. My father moved there for just that reason. He couldn't stand the limitations placed on black men in America. Much like Rose in your story, he wanted to be a man and not a black man.

In a perfect world, the words of our founding fathers would hold true: ". . . that all men are created equal, that they are endowed by their Creator with certain unalienable rights, that among these are life, liberty and the pursuit of happiness."

But for the average Negro in America, life and liberty are concepts wrought with struggle and segregation. And happiness, though endowed from our Creator, is little more than a concept.

You have been fortunate to be able to see another side of life. It gives you insight and perspective few black people have ever experienced. But you can't forget where you came from. Think about the way your mother and father toiled to give you the best they could. And though the legacy they left you isn't tangible like a luxurious cottage in the woods, it's deep and ancient like waters of the Nile. And if you lose that in your writing, you have become the literary equivalent of a tasteless dinner.

We all would love to have a serene place for reflection and relaxation. But I must ask you, what is the likelihood that Eleanor would repeat the same scene in a dinner club on Park Avenue? Would she include you with the other wives at their country club? I fear not. Try as she may to be a genuine friend, your relationship will always be unequal. I know many blacks who have acquired money and prestige but can never shake off the stigma of being black. They try to create a world for themselves where color doesn't matter, but it always matters. And if we aren't honest about it, we're not only denying our brethren, we are denying who we are.

Cora, you are a beautiful, smart black woman. Don't lose that in your writing. Tell the story of the strength and perseverance that courses through your veins. Don't strive to be a great writer. Be a great black writer.

Respectfully,

Langston

August 4, 1928 (Chesterfield County)

When Eleanor first brought over my journal and a pen, I couldn't fathom having a desire to write. I couldn't find words. There was too much whirling around in my head. But I now see I have to write, or I will go mad staring at these walls. It's amazing how many lies were told so that I could come here. I shouldn't be surprised things are in such a shamble.

A few days ago, Eleanor and I were at the soda shop helping Margaret paint. Around suppertime, we returned to the cottage. Eleanor went down to the cellar for a bottle of wine while I made some sandwiches. As I was slicing the tomatoes, I remembered the letter from Langston I picked up from the post office. I sat down at the kitchen table to read it. His reaction broke my heart. When Eleanor returned from the cellar, I was sobbing.

"Cora, what is it? Are the children all right?" she asked.

I handed her the letter.

She sat down next to me and read it. "What gives him the right to dictate what you write about? That story was good, Cora. And I don't give a damn what that son of a bitch says," she hissed as she flung the letter across the table.

"He's a respected poet," I said. "He's been published in several magazines, and not just in Negro magazines. He knows what works and what doesn't."

"He's a man, Cora. They all believe the only way to do anything is their way."

"What made me think I could be a writer?" I groaned.

Eleanor picked up the pages of the story Langston had returned in his letter. "You wrote this. You are a writer."

"I wasted my time and your money."

Eleanor sat the pages of the story down on the table and then gave me a hug. "It's only one opinion. One lousy opinion."

"I don't know about that."

"Come on, let's go sit out by the lake. You'll feel better," she said, grabbing the wine bottle and a couple of glasses.

Neither one of us thought about the sandwiches on the counter. We sat in the Adirondack chairs by the lake and drank wine in silence. The haunting call of the loons floated across the lake like a salve, quieting my thoughts. I felt a sense of peace ripple through me like the purple and pink shimmers of sunlight across the lake. Suddenly a loud noise came from the house. We both bolted up from our chairs. Eleanor thought it might be a raccoon or something in the garbage. I grabbed an oar from next to the canoe. I'm not sure what I planned to do. It was a lot heavier than I thought it would be, but I figured we needed something to scare whatever it was away. To our surprise, Mr. Fitzgerald stood in the middle of the kitchen reading the pages we had left on the table.

"What is this," he asked, holding them up in the air.

"Arthur, for goodness' sake. You frightened us," Eleanor said, stepping around me.

His expression changed from annoyed to darn right angry as he watched Eleanor sway across the floor.

"You should have let me know you were coming, dear. I would have had Cora prepare dinner for you," she said as she approached him.

"I was under the impression you were up here alone," he said, eyes fixed on me.

"Oh. You remember Cora. She replaced Agnes back in the city. She's up here to help with the house since Catherine has the summer off. Surely you didn't expect me to trouble you with such trivial details."

"This doesn't look like housekeeping to me," he said, shaking the paper tightly gripped in his fist. "More like a den of degradation and filth."

I wanted to grab my story, but I stood frozen watching Eleanor reach for the papers.

"Oh Arthur, don't be so melodramatic. A few papers strewn across the table hardly constitutes degradation or filth." She took the papers out of his hand and stacked them into a pile with the others. "Cora, I asked you to pick these things up off the table," she said without turning to look at me.

I leaned the oar against the back wall, wishing there had been a raccoon. Mr. Fitzgerald watched me closely as I passed by him to collect my papers from Eleanor.

"You know damn well I'm not talking about those papers. Have you no self-respect?" he hissed.

"I know I'm too lenient with the help, but let's not quarrel. You must be exhausted from your trip," she said as she patted his shoulder.

"Don't be coy with me, Eleanor," he said as he grabbed her hand. "I know what's going on up here." He pulled a thick manila envelope out of his breast pocket and tossed it on the table.

Eleanor turned to me and said, "That will be all, Cora."

"Yes, ma'am," I said, not knowing exactly where to go or what to do with the papers in my hands. I knew that things would only get worse if I retreated to my room on the second floor. So, I slipped out the kitchen door. As the screen banged against the frame, Mr. Fitzgerald began bombarding Eleanor with questions. I walked back around to the lake, but I could still hear every word.

The rise and fall of their voices reminded me of the nights I spent as a child listening to my parents. It always started with the boom of my father's voice and eventually grew into cries from Mama indicating his frustration had turned to rage. Though I never actually saw him strike her, I heard the crackling of her skin under his blows and the thuds of her body against the wall or into furniture. I'd cower on the floor between my bed and the wall, afraid to move, but even more fearful of what might happen if I did nothing. Eventually it would stop. My mother would get in bed with me. I would pretend to be asleep as I listened to her whimper. The next morning, he would leave before any of us woke up, and she would be sullen but quiet. I hated him for what he did to her, but I hated her too for provoking him.

I tried to think about other things, but Mr. Fitzgerald's voice echoed through the stillness of night like thunder. Eleanor's voice, throaty and strained, reflected none of the confidence I had seen the last few weeks. Oddly enough, the way they argued about money reminded me of my own marriage. I guess having more money doesn't make it easier. Either way it's about who has control. And that was the core issue with the Fitzgeralds.

Eleanor's attorney changed the terms of her trust fund so that Mr. Fitzgerald was no longer the executor. He discovered the change when he tried to make a withdrawal. And to make matters worse, Eleanor used some money from their joint account to purchase the soda shop. Fortunately, the money she gave me never came up. Maybe it wasn't enough for them to worry about.

It started to get cold outside. I contemplated how to grab my sweater without being seen or interrupting. I knew there was no way, but it gave me something to focus on other than what they were saying to one another. But then I heard my name.

"Cora doesn't have anything to do with this."

"Doesn't she? I shudder to think of the two of you up here for weeks all alone, lounging by the lake drinking wine and whatnot."

Mr. Fitzgerald called Eleanor and I deviants and threatened to have us both arrested. Tears stung in my eyes. I knew somehow, someway, I would be blamed for something. I wanted to leave before things got worse, but there wasn't any place for me to go. But before I could work myself into a tizzy, Eleanor's tone changed.

"We're friends."

"Is that what you and those jezebels down in Greenwich Village call it? Friends? And to think I thought you were just frigid."

"Frigid, huh. Charles doesn't think so," Eleanor snorted.

"That son of a bitch lawyer of yours?"

"Yes, and he's more of a man than you will ever be."

I held my breath and waited. And for a brief moment there was nothing. The sound of his hand slapping her face echoed in the darkness.

She didn't scream or cry. Her voice strong and determined, she said, "Go ahead, hit me again if it makes you feel better, but it won't change anything. You'll still be a weak man who needs my trust fund to survive. Well, I won't be used anymore. I am divorcing you and taking my money with me. Maybe one of your little whores can support you."

"You vindictive bitch," he said.

And then there was a shatter of glass and crack of wood. I sat on the edge of my chair unsure what to do. Even though they were two wealthy white folks I barely knew, it felt as if I was a child again. Eleanor's screams became my mother's. Each bump or crash shuddered through my body. My mother's black eyes and the bruises on Agnes's pale face flashed through my mind. The next thing I knew I was at the back door, oar in hand.

When I opened the door, I saw Mr. Fitzgerald straddling Eleanor's body, choking her. I ran toward them with the oar raised and whacked him on the side of his head so hard it knocked him out. He collapsed on top of her. Without even thinking I rolled him off and pulled Eleanor up.

She grabbed me and hugged me.

"Oh my God," she gasped with blood dripping from her nose.

"Come on, we can't stay here," I said, grabbing a table scarf off the floor for her nose. "Can you walk?"

She nodded.

We scrambled outside. Eleanor lagged behind. I couldn't tell if she was hurt, but we didn't have time to inspect her injuries. I wanted to be as far away from the cottage as possible when he woke up. I put my arm around her waist and told her to lean into me. Together we hobbled like two people in a three-legged race up the hill toward town. I kept looking over my shoulder, expecting him to come after us.

The road to town was deserted and dark. The pounding of our feet through the gravel alerted someone's dog, setting off a chorus of barking. I wanted to walk faster, but Eleanor kept stopping to catch her breath. What generally took us a half hour dragged on for what felt like hours.

When we reached the edge of town, all the houses along the perimeter were dark. I knew people turned in early but hoped someone would be milling around — but the streets were empty. I longed for the noise and commotion of Lenox Avenue.

The upstairs apartment of the soda shop was dark. I had no idea what we would do if Margaret didn't answer. Fortunately, it only took two quick raps before she flung open the screen door. She took one look at Eleanor and ushered us inside.

"Did he follow you?" she asked as she switched off the light and locked the door.

"I don't think so," I said, not sure whether I should tell her about hitting him in the head with the canoe oar.

Once we were up in the apartment, Margaret quickly pulled the shades down and drew the curtains. In the light, Eleanor looked almost as bad as Agnes did a few months ago. White women bruise very easily.

I led Eleanor to the davenport while Margaret gathered towels and Mercurochrome from the washroom. We quietly attended to her wounds and then helped her into bed. Once she was settled, Margaret and I went back downstairs to the restaurant kitchen.

"What happened?"

"Mr. Fitzgerald showed up. He wasn't supposed to be back until the end of the month. They argued over the recent changes to her trust fund." I didn't feel right about sharing the other details of their argument but I decided to tell her about hitting him with the canoe oar.

"He came in right after you and Eleanor left. I thought for sure you all had seen him. He had a chocolate sundae but seemed preoccupied. When he finished, he looked around and shook his head. I thought it was odd that he didn't say anything about owning the shop, but I figured the money wasn't a big deal to him."

"More than you would think."

"Enough to do that to her?"

"It wasn't just the money."

"It never is. Somehow, someway she pushed him. At least that's what my husband would say whenever he hit me. They get mad and there is nothing we can do about it. A man does whatever he wants to his wife. No one gives a damn."

I suddenly remembered that afternoon Eleanor and I had the conversation about Agnes. She had fiddled with the sleeve of her dress. I remember thinking it was too warm for long-sleeved dresses, but I just figured it was one of the peculiarities of white women. It never occurred to me she was the one hiding behind propriety and pretending things were all right.

"You know he'll come straight here looking for you."

"I know."

"You should take the seven o'clock train back to the city in the morning."

"I'm not running away," I said.

Margaret pursued her lips and shook her head.

"I had to do something. I couldn't stand by and watch him strangle her."

"No one gives a damn how a man treats his wife, much less that a darkie wants to help her," she said.

The word darkie surprised me. She had never made any reference to the color of my skin. And though it wounded my feelings, I knew she was right. Neither one of us noticed Eleanor standing in the doorway.

"She's right. No one wants to hear that. The only thing that matters now is that you knocked Arthur in the head with the oar. I'll go back to the cottage and reason with him," she said.

"You can't go back there," Margaret interjected.

"I have to. Otherwise, he'll have the sheriff here first thing in the morning to arrest Cora. And I can't let that happen."

"It's not safe," I said.

"It will be if Margaret comes with me. He would never do anything with someone there."

I opened my mouth to point out that I was there and it hadn't stopped him, but then the colored cook didn't count.

"And if that doesn't work?" I asked.

She signed heavily. "It has to."

Margaret didn't want to get involved but agreed nonetheless to go back to the cottage. I sat at the kitchen table with my eyes fixed on the second hand of the clock from the moment they left. Thirty minutes passed before the glow of headlights drew me to the window. The tension in my stomach tightened as I watched Margaret park the truck. I glanced back down the road expecting to see more headlights, but there was no one else. Eleanor carried my notebook and papers. Margaret followed behind with my satchel. The ashen look on both of their faces told me all I needed to know. I crumpled into the chair beside me, burying my face in my hands.

"No. No. No," I sobbed. Mr. Fitzgerald had been kind to me the few times I interacted with him. I never meant to hurt him.

Eleanor knelt in front of me and held my hands. "It was an accident."

"You had to do something," Margaret said from across the room.

"I didn't mean to . . ."

"Shh. I know," Eleanor replied through her own tears as she pulled me into her arms. We held each other and cried. Finally, Eleanor stood up, wiped her eyes and took a deep breath. "I'm sending you home."

I looked up at her, unable to completely comprehend what she had just said. "What?" I asked.

"I'm sending you home on the seven o'clock train. Once you're gone, I'll alert the sheriff. That way you will be long gone before he starts asking questions. My face will explain everything. Trust me, they will be as anxious as we are to put this behind us," she said.

Her calmness frightened me. Her husband was dead and she was talking about it like someone neglected to take out the garbage.

"Won't people think it's odd if I just disappear?" I asked.

"It's a vacation town. People are always coming and going. No one will notice you're gone."

"Trust me, they'll notice. Especially once the news of Mr. Fitzgerald's death is made public," I explained, knowing that she was oblivious to the way people watched me at the general store.

She sighed. "Well, first thing in the morning I want you to go to the general store and make a lot of noise about being sent home early. Tell them Arthur sent you away last night and Margaret was kind enough to let you stay. Make a scene so people don't forget."

I imagined myself as one of those loud, lowlife Negroes. The ones who make everyone think we're all ignorant. And it occurred to me I wouldn't have to do much to make the people believe me. They expected me to act that way anyway. I could slip away and leave the entire nightmare behind. No matter how much education I have or how I carry myself, to them I was still just a dumb nigger, like all the rest. It might save my life, but everything I ever lived for would die. And that would be worse than anything they could do to me.

I wiped the tears off my face and stood up. "I can't do that. I won't do that."

"Cora, you have to. It's the only way we can make this go away."

"Eleanor, I never thought a white woman and a black woman could have a real friendship, but you have been one of the best friends I have ever had. You understand me in ways no one ever has. But there is still a big difference between us. People see you and they assume the best. They want to make the world right for you. They see me and assume the worst. They are just waiting for confirmation of every negative thing they have ever thought of colored people. The proper language and appropriate dress is the act to them. And if I do what you suggested it would be worse than walking into one of those lakes and drowning myself. I'd be drowning my entire race."

She sank into the chair and bowed her head.

"There is no use trying to figure a way out of this. I'll go to the sheriff and confess," I said.

"They will arrest you," Eleanor said.

"I know, but what else can I do," I said, trying hard to hide my fear. The police have always terrified me. They treat Negroes like rebellious runaway slaves.

Eleanor and I left Margaret's place and walked over to the sheriff's house. She rang the bell several times before he came to the door, his wife trailing behind him. He invited us in, and we sat down at the kitchen table. I explained the whole thing to him while his wife made a pot of coffee. The sheriff listened patiently despite Eleanor's constant interruptions.

"Ralph, if she hadn't intervened, I'd be the one dead at the cottage. She's a hero, not a criminal," she pleaded, unable to stop the tears.

The sheriff ignored her and looked me straight in the eye. "You know I have to arrest you."

I nodded.

"But I suppose we ought to go out to the house first. May, call Dr. Thompson and tell him to meet me over at the jailhouse," he said as he stood up.

Eleanor followed him close behind arguing. "This is all Arthur's fault. He started all this trouble. You have to listen."

"Mrs. Fitzgerald, you're lucky I'm not locking you up, too, as an accomplice," he said.

The three of us walked to a tiny square building on the opposite edge of town, across the street from the church. The sheriff turned on the lights and led me to the back of the building where there were two cells.

"Is this really necessary?" Eleanor asked.

"Mrs. Fitzgerald, I'm warning you," the sheriff replied.

"Don't worry, Cora. Margaret called Charles. He'll be here first thing in the morning," she said as she wrapped her arms around me. "Everything is going to be okay. I promise."

As the metal of the cell door clanged shut, something seized up in my chest as the sound of my heartbeat thrashed in my ear. Right and wrong no longer mattered as my conviction crumbled. I just wanted to go home. As I paced back and forth in the cell, I questioned why it had been so easy to risk everything on a scant chance at becoming a real writer. I wasn't like the others, and I knew that. They didn't have husbands and children. They could afford to live for their art. But I was blinded by my desire to be a part of their world, and as a result I could lose the only world that mattered. My discontent could cost me not only my family but my freedom.

When I finally sat down on the cot, the image of Mr. Fitzgerald sprawled on the ground flashed through my mind. Why hadn't I just screamed or thrown something at him? There had to have been another way to stop him. The next morning when the sun filtered through the tiny window in the cell, I realized I had missed the sunrise, but I didn't care. I just stared at the wall.

The gray thick blocks reminded me of the basement walls in my building back home. I hated the dampness and the way the sun filtered through the narrow windows casting shadows on the walls. I felt imprisoned down there. But those days seem like heaven as I sit here in this cell. What was so bad about taking care of my family? Why wasn't I satisfied in my own kitchen?

August 7, 1928 (Chesterfield County)

I've been staring at these walls the last six days, asking myself why I was so unhappy. What was so burdensome about being a wife and mother? It was foolish to risk my family for a whimsical dream. If only I had been honest with Earl about the writing. I could have told him about the letters between Langston and me. What was I afraid of? It wasn't like there was anything intimate about our relationship. Maybe he would have supported my efforts to enter the contest. Maybe I wouldn't have had to come up here. I tried writing him a letter, but he deserves to hear it directly from me. I called the house yesterday when the sheriff allowed me to use the telephone, but no one answered. It's probably for the best. Hearing Earl's voice would only make it that much harder to be here. I'm barely sleeping as it is. And though Margaret sends food over every day, I haven't had much of an appetite.

I miss my family. What if I never see them again?

August 10, 1928 (Chesterfield County)

Yesterday afternoon, I heard heavy footsteps coming down the hallway. I assumed they had come to transfer me to the county jail, but Mr. Gaston was with the sheriff.

"You're free to go," the sheriff said, opening the cell.

I thought I was dreaming. I didn't move.

Mr. Gaston came into the cell and reached out his hand. "Come on, Cora. Eleanor is waiting for you at Margaret's," he said.

I looked from his face to the sheriff's. The sheriff nodded.

I wanted to ask why, but I just followed them out of the cell. I expected to see a crowd of people waiting and sneering outside the jailhouse, but there was no one. In fact, as I walked with Mr. Gaston back to Margaret's, no one so much as looked in my direction. Eleanor and Margaret were at the kitchen table, drinking coffee.

"I'm so glad you are all right. I hated leaving you there so long," Eleanor said as she rushed to me.

I was still too stunned to ask what had happened or why they had let me go. None of it felt real to me. Margaret insisted I sit down and eat. While she fixed me a sandwich, Mr. Gaston explained everything that happened. When the sheriff and the town doctor arrived at the cottage that night, they saw the broken table and shattered glass. The doctor, a close family friend, was more interested in attending to Eleanor's injuries than examining the body. After a bit of coercion from the sheriff, the doctor examined Mr. Fitzgerald and deemed his death an accident.

"He probably lost his balance and hit his head when he crashed into the table," he said.

Though the sheriff told him I had confessed, the doctor refused to sign the death certificate as anything other than an accident. The sheriff insisted on following procedure which included going before the judge to determine probable cause for arrest. Eleanor had Mr. Gaston draw up a sizable anonymous donation to the town's beautification fund. When they met in front of the judge Thursday morning, everyone knew about the donation. No one wanted to drag the town or the Fitzgerald family through the unpleasantness of a trial, especially since it would have to include what Mr. Fitzgerald had done to Eleanor. His death was ruled an accident. Today's newspaper headline reads: "Bank President killed in early morning canoe accident."

It all feels unreal. Especially the fact that I killed someone. My heart is broken. I wish there had been another way. Eleanor wanted me to come back to the cottage with her, but I couldn't. Fortunately, Margaret invited me to stay at her place until I leave on the 20th. I just want to go home.

August 11, 1928 (Chesterfield County)

I talked to Earl last night and told him everything. Talking about the writing stuff was almost as hard as telling him about Mr. Fitzgerald. His only questions were about Langston and me. I assured him there was never anything romantic or intimate between us. What surprised me the most was his belief that had I not protected Eleanor I also might have died. I hadn't thought about that.

The other strange thing was I couldn't tell if my story made him angry. He was uncharacteristically reserved. He did, however, seem relieved that I wasn't staying at the cottage anymore. The conversation felt strained, but I guess that's to be expected. There was a lot to digest in a single phone call. Hopefully Earl will be able to forgive me one day, though I don't know if I will ever forgive myself.

I spent today upstairs in the apartment. I didn't feel up to interacting with anyone. When Margaret came up after closing the shop, she had a telegram for me from Earl. I was certain that I had lost him and my family, but instead it said: *Wish you had trusted me with your dreams. Please come home. The rest doesn't matter.*

Eleanor stopped by after supper. I told her I decided to take the seven o'clock train back to the city tomorrow rather than wait until the 20th. She tried to convince me to wait until the weekend so that we could travel together. She was heading back to make final arrangements for the funeral before her mother-in-law and children returned from Europe. But I didn't want to wait. I wanted to go home. She offered to pay for my ticket, but I've taken enough money from her. It's time to go back to my own life.

August 26, 1928 (New York, New York)

I haven't felt much like writing the last two weeks. Being home has been enough. Up until Junior and Dorothy came back, I'd go to the club with Earl. Now the children and I seem content sitting in the parlor together listening to the radio until it's time for bed. Last night, as I was washing dishes, I felt so grateful to be standing over my own sink. Even the heavy footsteps overhead and voices floating in through the open window were welcomed. When I looked up, Earl was standing in the doorway watching me.

"I'm glad you're home," he said.

"Me too."

He sat down at the kitchen table. "I've been thinking about that story you wrote."

I grabbed the dish towel on the counter and dried my hands. "I'm sorry about all of that."

"It's a good story," he continued, ignoring my apology. "You should enter that contest."

I sat in the chair across from him. "I just want all of that stuff behind us, especially now that the children are back from Georgia," I said.

"Send it," he said, standing up.

"I don't know."

"You owe it to yourself," he said as he kissed me on the top of my head.

I sat there thinking about what he said for a while. I had risked losing everything to be able to write. What was the point if I didn't see it through? I had to at least try. After the children went to bed, I pulled the story out, made a few changes and retyped it. Today on the way to work I stopped at the post office. Just as I was about to hand the letter to the postmaster, I was seized by fear. But then I remembered a passage in *The Awakening*. Mademoiselle Reisz had put her arms around Edna, felt her shoulder blades, and said, "The bird that would soar above the level plain of tradition and prejudice must have strong wings."

I had spent so much time thinking about what led Edna to walk into the ocean, not once considering what I could do to soar above all that burdened me. I mailed the story to *Opportunity*. No matter what happens I will be stronger for trying.

New York, New York
October 20, 1928

Dear Langston,

I did not think I would ever write to you again after I received your last letter. In my mind that letter will always be the very thing that set off a chain of events that led to the worst night of my life. Though I do not feel it necessary to share those details, I would like to articulate why I found your words so disturbing.

Over the months of our correspondence, I grew to depend on your opinion and advice. You inspired me. Our conversations awakened a part of me I thought was long dead. You taught me how to observe my world. You gave me a stage to voice my thoughts. The world began to open in ways I didn't expect. I began to notice the birds in the garden and the shape of trees as I walked through the park. I saw similarities between nature and myself. I began to ask questions. I started to see the beauty of the world, but I also saw the ugliness. Most of that ugliness centered around racism and the way Negroes are treated in America. But I can't write about issues of race and ignore issues of sex.

Over the years I have seen too many women, colored and white, mistreated and constrained simply because they are women. And while I understand colored women don't have the same voice as white women, I can't turn my back on any woman. I believe all women must stand together if any woman wants to get ahead. That is probably true of people in general, but women tend to work together better. Unfortunately, that belief got me into a heap of trouble with the law. I tried to help another woman and ended up almost ruining my own life. But I don't have any regrets. I suspect I would react in the same way if I were presented with a similar situation again. What's important to me is that women are treated with the same unalienable rights that are afforded to men.

You suggested I write about what it meant to stand alongside the black man. But that isn't the only story. Nor is privilege and education something to be ashamed of, because as a woman, they don't necessarily make your life any easier. The stories that are important to me are about what it means to be a woman in a world that neither respects your body nor your mind. Those stories reminded me of Walt Whitman.

Whenever I have read "Song of Myself" the focus has always been on the pleasures of heaven and the pain of hell. But now I see that isn't as important as the following stanza: "I am the poet of the woman the same as the man, And I say it is as great to be a woman as to be a man ..." I am a writer for women the same as for blacks. It doesn't make me a greater writer to focus solely on blacks. Nor does that mean I should focus solely on women. I belong to both equally. And as a writer I have no choice but to write from the perspective of both. But if I must choose, I will stand with Whitman, "And I say there is nothing greater than the mother of men."

I am eternally grateful for your time and advice. It helped me to become a better writer. Best of luck with the publication of your book.

Sincerely,

Cora James

November 1, 1928

It's been a while since I've written in my journal. It hasn't felt as important. But today I had the urge when I picked up the mail. There was a letter from Eleanor. She and the children have moved to San Francisco, California, to be as far away as possible from New York. She wrote about the expansiveness of the mountains and proximity to the sea. She said it's all that she needs to live a contented life. There was no mention of Mr. Gaston. She did however invite me to come for a visit. She said there was a room with a view of the sea that would be perfect for writing. And for a moment I imagined the waves crashing against the shore and a writing desk by the window, but I knew I would never take her up on her offer. I'd come too close to drowning before.

There was also a letter from *Opportunity*. It thanked me for my interest in their contest but informed me my story wasn't selected. I'm disappointed but not surprised. Maybe I'll try again next year.

CORA'S READING LIST

Brontë, Charlotte. *Jane Eyre*. 1847.

Chopin, Kate. *The Awakening*. 1899.

Dixon, Franklin, W. *The Missing Chums*. 1928.

Du Bois, W. E. B. *The Souls of Black Folk*. 1903.

Dunbar, Paul. *The Sport of the Gods*. 1902.

Fauset, Jessie Redmon. *Plum Bun*. 1928.

Fauset, Jessie Redmon. *There Is Confusion*. 1924.

Hughes, Langston. "Cross." *The Weary Blues*. 1926.

Hughes, Langston. "The Negro Speaks of Rivers." 1921.

Hughes, Langston. "Troubled Woman." *The Weary Blues*. 1926.

Hughes, Langston. *The Weary Blues*. 1926.

Larsen, Nella. *Quicksand*. 1928.

Van Vechten, Carl. *Nigger Heaven*. 1926.

West, Dorothy. "The Typewriter." 1926.

Whitman, Walt. *Leaves of Grass*. 1855.

Whitman, Walt. "Song of Myself." *Leaves of Grass*. 1855.

Whitman, Walt. *Specimen Days and Collect*. 1882.

ACKNOWLEDGMENTS

Cora's Kitchen was a labor of love written to hold space for women who had neither the time, resources, or opportunity to live their creative dreams. I am so thankful I had the opportunity and a village of people who supported and encouraged me to live mine.

I want to thank my Goddard College faculty advisors, Aimee Lui, Nicola Morris, and Reikko Rizzuto, for their expert knowledge of craft, guiding me through the early stages of writing this novel, and for teaching me what it means to be a writer in the world. To all the Goddard peeps who offered advice, encouragement, and support throughout the writing process, I am so honored to have you as my writing tribe. To Debbie Staley for making me accept myself as a writer and for always being a phone call away.

Thanks to Anna Leahy, Doug Dechow, Patricia King, and Mary Cantrell for their early reading and deep analysis of Cora's story. To Rosemary Daniell and the women of the Zona Rosa for welcoming me into their group and championing Cora's Kitchen. Rosemary, thank you for pushing me to enter the William Faulkner – William Wisdom Creative Writing Competition and for being there as only another mother could.

I also want to thank Luciana Ricciutelli for encouraging me to send her the manuscript and subsequently accepting it for publication with Inanna Publications. My heart aches that we didn't get to work together. You are deeply missed. To Ashley Rayner for picking up the manuscript and seeing it through edits and scheduling changes. You were a woman of your word. To Renée Knapp, Brenda Cranney, and the entire Inanna Publication staff for gracefully working through adversity and loss.

I would also like to acknowledge and thank my publicist, Caitlin Hamilton-Summie, for believing in Cora's story and sticking with me through the long, bumpy road to publication.

To my children, Matt, Nick, and Kelsey, for all the ways you have encouraged me and kept me grounded. I love you more than words can express.

And to the love of my life, Michael, you have always been there. Thank you for your willingness to do whatever was needed and for loving me through it all.

And to Him who is able to do far more abundantly than all that we ask or think, according to the power at work within us, to Him be the glory.

Credit: Francesco Fedeli

Kimberly Garrett Brown is the publisher and executive editor of Minerva Rising Press, an independent women's literary press. She has an MFA in Creative Writing and an MS in Written Communication. Her publications include *The Rumpus, Women Writers, Women's Books, Linden Avenue Literary Journal, Black Lives Have Always Mattered: A Collection of Essays, Poems and Personal Narratives, The Feminine Collective*, and the *Chicago Tribune*. She currently lives in Boca Raton, Florida.

p.5 - Walt Whitman <u>Leaves of Grass</u>
"Song of Myself"